"Why do you think someone wants to harm you?" he asked.

"I witnessed a crime."

They turned a corner and he stopped short.

"What?" She looked around him.

A stranger was coming out of Will's cabin.

"Do you recognize him?" she said.

"No." He motioned to a nearby tree. "Hide back there. I'll check it out."

"It could be dangerous."

"Or simply a hiker lost in the mountains. Kinda like you." Will smiled and nodded toward the tree. "Go on."

"Maybe you should take this." She offered him the gun.

An odd smile creased his lips. "Thanks, but you keep it."

She nodded and watched him walk away, shielding herself behind the tree. From this vantage point she could watch the scene unfold, not that she had a great escape plan.

Suddenly, a gunshot echoed across the property.

An eternal optimist, **Hope White** was born and raised in the Midwest. She and her college sweetheart have been married for thirty years and are blessed with two wonderful sons, two feisty cats and a bossy border collie. When not dreaming up inspirational tales, Hope enjoys hiking, sipping tea with friends and going to the movies. She loves to hear from readers, who can contact her at hopewhiteauthor@gmail.com.

Books by Hope White

Love Inspired Suspense

Echo Mountain

Mountain Rescue
Covert Christmas
Payback
Christmas Undercover

Hidden in Shadows
Witness on the Run
Christmas Haven
Small Town Protector
Safe Harbor

Visit the Author Profile page at Harlequin.com.

CHRISTMAS UNDERCOVER

HOPE WHITE

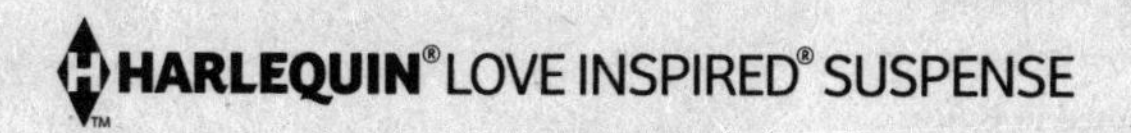

If you purchased this book without a cover you should be aware that this book is stolen property. It was reported as "unsold and destroyed" to the publisher, and neither the author nor the publisher has received any payment for this "stripped book."

Recycling programs for this product may not exist in your area.

LOVE INSPIRED BOOKS™

ISBN-13: 978-0-373-44698-8

Christmas Undercover

This edition published by arrangement with Love Inspired Books.

www.Harlequin.com

Printed in U.S.A.

May the God of hope fill you with all joy and peace
as you trust in Him, so that you may overflow with hope
by the power of the Holy Spirit.

—*Romans* 15:13

This book is dedicated to Mark Jamieson of the Seattle PD,
who generously answers my many questions.

ONE

FBI agent Sara Vaughn awoke with a start, her heart pounding against her chest. Darkness surrounded her and it took a second for her eyes to adjust.

Panic took hold. No, she was beyond that. She'd outgrown it.

She counted to three, taking a deep breath, then exhaled. She clicked on her headlamp. Tall, majestic evergreen trees stretched up toward the starlit sky.

The mountains. She was in the Cascade Mountains following a lead that her supervisor, Greg Bonner, said was a waste of time.

Sara knew better.

The sound of deep male voices echoed from beyond a cluster of trees to her left.

"Be reasonable, David!" a man shouted.

David Price was one of the three business partners who were on this mountain getaway. The other men were Victor LaRouche and Ted Harrington, and together they owned the drug company LHP, Inc.

Sara made her way toward the sound of raised voices.

She was proud of herself for managing to get on the trail guide team hired to lead them up Echo Mountain. This isolated spot in the Cascade Mountains of Washington would surely give the men the privacy they needed to solidify their plan.

Getting a dangerous drug into the hands of unsuspecting consumers.

"Why do you have to make this so hard?"

She recognized Vic LaRouche's voice because of its Southern twang.

She stayed off the main trail, not wanting to alert them to her presence, and made her way through the brush. Edging around a large boulder, she stepped over a fallen branch in silence. She needed to stay invisible, hidden. Something she was good at.

The men were no doubt having this discussion a safe distance away from the lead guide, Ned, so as not to wake him. It didn't take much to wake Sara. Even in sleep, she was always on alert.

"It's not right and you both know it," David said.

"It was an anomaly, a mistake," Ted Harrington said.

"A mistake that could kill people."

"Don't be dramatic," LaRouche said.

This was it—the evidence she'd been looking for.

She pulled out her phone, hoping to record some of their conversation. If she could catch them admitting to their plan, it would go a long way to proving she was right, that she wasn't just an "overzealous" agent trying to prove something.

She crept closer, shielding herself behind a towering western hemlock. Digging her fingers into the bark, she peeked around the tree. The three men hovered beside a small campfire, the flames illuminating their faces. LaRouche and Harrington were tall, middle-aged men, older than David Price by at least ten years.

"I'm not in business to hurt people," David said.

"We're helping people, sport," Harrington said, slapping David's shoulder. "Letting them sleep like they never have before."

"And they don't wake up."

"That hasn't been irrefutably proved," Harrington said.

"Even one death is too many."

LaRouche, a tall, regal-looking man, jumped into the conversation. It grew into a shouting match, giving Sara the chance to sneak even closer. She darted to another tree, only ten feet from the men.

She clicked off her headlamp.

Hit the video record button on her phone.

And held her breath.

"I didn't sign on for this!" David said.

"Majority rules," Harrington countered.

"Then, I'm out. I'll sell you my share of the company."

Harrington threw up his hands and paced a few steps away.

"If you leave, stock prices go down," LaRouche said calmly.

"I don't care. Some things are more important than money."

"Like your family?" LaRouche taunted.

"Is that a threat?" David said.

"Sure, why not?"

David lunged at LaRouche. Harrington dived in between them. "Enough!"

The two men split apart, David glaring at his partners.

"Calm down. Let's talk this through," Harrington said.

"Talk? You mean threaten me?" David said.

"I like to think of it as persuading you, David," LaRouche countered.

"No, I'm done." David started to walk away.

It seemed as if the conversation was over.

Then LaRouche darted around the fire, grabbed David's arm and flung him…

Over the edge of the trail.

The chilling sound of a man crying out echoed across the mountains.

Sara gasped and took a step backward.

A twig snapped beneath her boot.

LaRouche and Harrington whipped their heads around and spotted her. They looked as stunned as she felt. The three of them stared at each other.

No one moved. She didn't breathe.

Heart racing, she watched the expression on LaRouche's face change from stunned to something far worse: the look of a murderer who was hungry for more.

"It was an accident," Harrington said.

LaRouche reached into his jacket, no doubt for a weapon.

In that millisecond, her only conscious thought was survival.

Sara clicked on her headlamp and took off, retracing her steps over the rugged terrain. She was outnumbered and couldn't retrieve her off-duty piece quick enough. She had to get safe and preserve the video evidence against them.

Shoving the phone in her pocket, she hopped a fallen branch and dodged the boulder on the other side. As she picked up speed, she heard a man grunt as he tripped and hit the ground behind her.

"Where are you going? We need your help!" Harrington called.

Beating back the tentacles of fear, she searched for a trail, or at least a more even surface. She'd left everything at the campsite but the clothes on her back, so her odds for survival weren't great, especially considering the cold temperatures in the mountains this time of year.

Stop going to that dark place, she scolded herself. She had to figure out how to contact her boss and report the murder before the men reported it as an accident.

Call her boss, right, the man who'd ordered her to take time off. He didn't even know she was chasing a lead he'd proclaimed was a dead end.

"David fell and we need your help!" Harrington yelled.

David fell? Is that what you call it when you fling a man off a cliff?

She sucked in the cool mountain air, pumping her arms, trying to get a safe distance away where she could get a cell signal and call for help.

"Let's talk about this!" Harrington pressed.

Like they'd "talked" to David Price? The memory of his desperate cry sent shivers across her shoulders.

She found the trail, but if she found it, so would they. They were taller than her five foot three, their strides longer. It wouldn't take them long to catch her.

And kill her.

They'd probably fabricate a story about how she was responsible for David's death. That would wrap everything up in a neat bow—just in time for Christmas.

No. She wouldn't let them win.

A gunshot echoed across the mountain range.

She bit back a gasp. How would they explain her body riddled with bullet holes? Unless they hoped wild animals would rip it apart, making cause of death that much harder to determine.

Suddenly she ran out of trail. She peered over the mountain's edge into the black abyss below.

"Think," she whispered.

She realized her rope was still hooked to her belt. She hadn't planned to drift off to sleep earlier, so she hadn't taken off her gear. She wrapped the rope around a tree root jutting out from the side of the mountain below the trail and pulled it tight.

For the first time in her life, she appreciated Uncle Matt's insistence that she take wilderness survival courses, along with self-defense. She used to think he'd forced her to take the classes because her small frame made her a target for bullies. She eventually realized it was because of the nightmares. He thought the classes would empower her, make her feel safe.

Sara had never felt safe.

She dropped to her stomach and shimmied over the edge. Clinging to the rope, she let herself down slowly, hoping to hit a ledge or plateau where she could wait it out. She clicked off her headlamp. At least if she could disappear for a few hours until sunrise, she might be able to make her way out of Echo Mountain State Park.

She calmed her breathing, questioning her decision to follow this lead on her own. Was her boss right? Was she too determined for her own good?

Sara gripped the rope with gloved hands and steadied herself against the mountainside with her boots.

"What do you want to do?" Harrington said.

His voice was close, right above her close. She held her breath.

"We'll send Bill to find her," LaRouche said. "He's got climbing experience."

"Wouldn't it be better if we—"

"No, we need answers, like who sent her and what she heard. Then she needs to disappear."

Disappear. They were determined to kill her. Sara's pulse raced against her throat.

As she hung there, suspended in midair, she searched her surroundings, trying to see something, trying to stay grounded.

All she could see was a wall of black, which reminded her of…

Stay in here and don't make a sound.

But, Daddy—

I mean it. Take care of your brother.

Suddenly someone tugged on the rope, yanking her out of the memory.

"Sara Long, is that you?" LaRouche said.

She was relieved they only knew her undercover name, Sara Long. That should keep them from discovering her true identity.

Then, suddenly, they started pulling her up. No, she wouldn't let them get away with it, killing people, innocent people.

Killing her.

She released the rope and grabbed the tree root, then

edged her way down the side of the mountain, grabbing onto whatever felt solid.

She grabbed onto a branch…

It pulled loose from the earth and she started to slide. Flailing her arms, she reached for something, anything, to slow her descent.

But it was too dark, and the fall too steep.

It wouldn't surprise the guys in her field office if she died out here like this: alone, on some rogue assignment gone south.

She didn't care. At least this time she'd taken on the enemy instead of hiding from him.

I'm sorry, Daddy. I should have done something to save you.

She came to a sudden stop. Her head whipped back, slammed against something hard, and she was swallowed by darkness.

Will Rankin approached the end of the trail and made the final turn. His breath caught in his throat at the stunning view, sunlight sparkling off the calm, turquoise water at the base of Echo Mountain, with the Cascade Mountain range spanning the horizon behind the lake. This was it, the perfect place to open his heart to God, hoping for peace to ease the resentment lingering in his heart.

Intellectually Will knew it was time to let it go for so many reasons, not the least of which being his daughters. They needed a loving, gentle father, not a bitter, angry one.

Will thought he had coped with Megan's death pretty well over the past two years, but the dark emotions continued to have a stronghold over his heart. He was still angry with his wife for shutting him out as she battled cancer, and he struggled with resentment about his mother-in-law, who challenged nearly every decision Will made about Claire and Marissa.

I love my girls so much, Lord. Isn't that enough?

Apparently not to his mother-in-law.

No, he wouldn't think about that today. Today he'd commune with nature and pray: for his daughters, for emotional peace and for the strength to get him through the upcoming Christmas season, the girls' second Christmas without their mom.

It was unseasonably warm at the base of the mountain. Although a recent light snowfall dusted the area around the lake with a layer of white, it would probably melt off by noon. He smiled, thinking about how much the girls were looking forward to playing in the snow.

Then something else caught his eye across the lake.

A splash of red.

Curious, he pulled out his binoculars and peered through the lenses. It looked like a woman in a red jacket, jeans and hiking boots. Her long brown hair was strewn across her face.

She looked unconscious, or worse.

Will shoved the binoculars into his pack and took off. He had to get to her, had to save her. He glanced at his cell phone. No signal.

Please, Lord, let me save her.

As he sped toward the unconscious woman, he wondered how she'd ended up here. Was she a day hiker who hadn't brought enough hydration? He didn't see a backpack near her body, yet even day hikers knew better than to head into the mountains without supplies since the weather could change in a flash.

By the time he reached the unconscious woman, his heart was pounding against his chest. He shucked his pack and kneeled to administer first aid. "Ma'am?"

She was unresponsive.

"Ma'am, can you hear me?"

What had happened to this fragile-looking creature? He wondered if she got separated from her party or had fallen off a trail above.

He gently brushed jet-black hair away from her face. She had color in her cheeks, a good sign. He took off his glove and pressed his fingers against her wrist to check her pulse.

"No!" She swung her arm, nailing Will in the face with something hard.

He jerked backward, stars arcing across his vision. He pinched his eyes shut against the pain. Gripping his nose, he felt blood ooze through his fingers. He struggled to breathe.

"Don't touch me!" she cried.

"I'm trying to help."

"Liar."

He cracked open his eyes. She towered above him, aiming a gun at his chest.

"Please," he said, putting out one hand in a gesture of surrender. "I'm sorry if I upset you, but I really do want to help."

"Yeah, help them kill me."

He noticed a bruise forming above her right eye and lacerations crisscrossing her cheek.

"You're hurt," he said.

"I'm fine."

Will guessed she was frightened and confused. Maybe even dehydrated.

"I'm Will Rankin, a volunteer with Echo Mountain Search and Rescue."

"Sure, and I'm Amelia Earhart."

"Check my pack. My driver's license is in the side pocket."

It was worth a try, although he knew all the sensible conversation in the world may not get through to someone in her condition.

Narrowing her eyes, she grabbed his backpack and stepped a few feet away. Never lowering the gun, she unzipped the side pocket.

"May I sit up to stop my nosebleed?" he asked.

She nodded that he could.

He would continue to act submissive so she wouldn't see him as a threat. It was the best way to keep her from firing the gun by accident. He sensed she wasn't a killer, but rather she was disoriented and frightened.

Sitting up, he leaned forward and pinched his nose, just below the bridge. He'd have dual black eyes for sure and didn't know how he'd explain that to his girls, or their grandparents.

You've got bigger problems than a bloody nose. He had to talk this woman down from her precarious ledge.

She rifled through his wallet and hesitated, fingering a photograph of Claire and Marissa.

"My girls," he said. "They're in first and third grades."

She shot him a look of disbelief and shoved his wallet and the photos haphazardly into his pack.

"Did you fall from a trail above?" he asked.

"I'm asking the questions!" She straightened and pointed the gun at his chest again. "And you'd better give me the right answers."

"Please," he said. "My girls… I'm all they've got. Their mother…died."

He thought he'd gotten through to her.

She flicked the gun. "Get up."

He slowly stood, realizing how petite she was, barely coming up to his chest.

"Where are they?" she demanded.

"Who?"

"LaRouche and Harrington."

"I'm sorry, but I don't know what you're talking about."

"Right, you randomly happened to find me."

"I did."

"Uh-huh. And you're out here, in the middle of nowhere, why?"

"I'm spending a few days in the mountains for—" he hesitated "—solitude."

"You're lying. There's more to it."

"I'm not lying, but you're right, there is more to it."

She waited and narrowed her eyes, expectant.

"I come to this spot by the lake to find emotional peace—" he hesitated "—with God's help."

"Yeah, right. Great story, *Will*."

He didn't miss the sarcastic pronunciation of his name, nor the paranoid look in her eye.

She dug in her jacket pocket and pulled out her phone. She frowned.

"You have a phone?" she asked.

"I do."

She shoved hers back into her pocket. "Give it to me."

He pulled it out, dropped it between them and raised his hands. "You won't get a signal here, but there's a spot by my cabin where I can usually find service."

"Your cabin?"

"I'm renting a cabin about a quarter of a mile north."

She eyed his phone, must have seen there weren't any bars, and shoved it into her other pocket.

"Let's go." When she picked up his pack, a groan escaped her lips.

"Do you want me to—"

"Walk," she demanded, her eyes watering.

They were obviously tears of pain. He guessed from the rip in her jacket and strained look on her face, she might have cracked a rib or two.

With a nod, he turned and headed toward the cabin. She was hurt and confused, and the worst part was, she wouldn't accept his help.

He'd have to rely on patience, kindness and compassion to make her feel safe. That would go a long way to ease her worry and earn her trust.

Hopefully that would be enough.

Sara wasn't sure how far she'd get before passing out from the excruciating pain of her headache, but she'd fight until she dropped. Shc had somehow survived the fall, and wouldn't allow herself to die at the hand of a hired thug.

It figures LaRouche and Harrington would send a handsome, clean-cut guy to find her—a real charmer, this one. Will or Bill or whatever his name was, had to be over six feet tall, with chestnut brown hair and green eyes, and he spoke with such a gentle, calming tone. What a story he'd crafted for himself: he'd come out here to pray?

He'd laid it on thick, all right. Those were probably his little girls in the photograph, girls who had no idea what their daddy did for a living.

In her ten years with the FBI, Sara had learned plenty about sociopaths and how they used their cunning intelligence and polished charisma to convince an interrogating agent of their innocence.

Clutching the gun, she took her finger off the trigger in case she stumbled and pulled it by accident. He wouldn't know the difference. As long as Will thought she aimed a gun at his back, he'd do as she ordered.

The trees around her started drifting in and out of focus. She blinked to clear her vision, and stumbled on a rock jutting out of the ground.

Strong, firm hands gripped her arms, keeping her upright. Will's green eyes studied her face, as if assessing her head injury. He must have realized his mistake, that he was still holding on to her, because his hands sprung free and he raised them, as if to say, *please don't shoot me.*

She stepped back and dropped the backpack on the ground. "It's throwing me off balance."

He picked up the pack and adjusted it across his shoulders with ease. "That bruise above your eye—" He hesitated. "Are you experiencing blurred vision?"

"I'm fine." She flicked the gun barrel toward the trail.

He continued walking.

"I have ice packs at the cabin," he said. "And pain reliever."

She hated that he was being so polite. It was an act, his

strategy to discover how much she knew. Those were La-Rouche and Harrington's orders, right?

Much like her official orders had been to leave it alone, put aside the LHP, Inc., investigation due to lack of evidence. But she'd pushed and pushed until Bonner had had enough, and told her to take a couple of weeks off.

So she did, and spent her vacation going undercover and buying her way on to the trail guide team that LaRouche, Harrington and Price had hired to take them up the mountain. Her goal: watch and listen, glean whatever information she could from the men who were on vacation with their guards down.

"Would you like some water?" Will offered.

She ignored him. Sara might be hurting, but she wasn't stupid. It would be too easy for Will to slip something into her water, rendering her unconscious.

"Guess not," he said softly.

She took a deep breath and bit back a gasp at the stab of bruised ribs. She decided it was a good thing because the pain would keep her conscious and alert.

He slowed down, closing the distance between them.

"Keep walking," she said through clenched teeth.

"I thought you might need to rest."

"I don't."

With what seemed like a frustrated sigh, he continued. Sure, he was frustrated. He wanted to finish this job quickly and move on to his next high-paying assignment.

She focused on his backpack as she struggled to place one foot in front of the other without losing her balance. It wasn't easy when she felt as though she'd stepped off the Tilt-A-Whirl at the county fair.

They continued in silence, her pulse ricocheting off the inside of her skull with each step. She had to make it, had to put these arrogant criminals behind bars.

She hoped they could pull the video recording off her

phone, even though she'd noticed it had been damaged in the fall.

Will's phone was working just fine. Maybe they were close to getting reception. She pulled his phone out of her pocket, but her trembling fingers dropped it. She snapped her gaze to Will, fearing he'd seen her weakness. He continued up the trail.

She waited until he was a good distance away and knelt down to retrieve the phone. When she stood, her vision blurred and she could barely make out Will's form. She squinted through the haze to see him.

He was no longer within sight.

She shoved the phone into her pocket and clutched the gun grip with both hands. Where did he go? Had he taken off up ahead, waiting to ambush her? She approached a sharp turn, blocked by a boulder.

Took a slow, shallow breath…

Darted around the corner.

And spotted Will, on his knees, with his hands interlaced behind his head.

"What are you doing?" she said.

"Waiting for you."

"Get up."

He stood, his back to her. "Are you all right?"

"Go on, keep moving."

He continued along the trail and she followed. He was waiting for her? More like he was messing with her head, and doing a good job of it.

"The cabin's not far," he said.

She ignored him, knowing how these guys worked. They insinuated themselves into your psyche and destroyed you from the inside out. This guy was luring her with his father-of-the-year, single-parent story. She'd seen the wallpaper on his phone of two adorable girls with strawberry blonde hair and big smiles. This guy was a master.

They trekked the rest of the way in silence, Sara focusing on breathing through the pain and shutting out the panic taunting her from the fringes of her mind. She was in the middle of nowhere with an assassin, and her next step could be her last.

No, she was tough. Even if others didn't believe it, she knew it in her heart.

If only she'd been tough when she was twelve.

They turned a corner to an open field with a cabin in the distance. Surely she'd be able to get a signal out there, in the middle of the field.

He marched in the direction of the cabin.

"Stop," she said. She'd be a fool to let him go inside with her. No doubt that was where he kept his tools of the trade—coercion tools.

"Sit down, over there." She jerked the gun barrel.

He sat down beside a fallen tree.

"You have rope in your pack?" she said.

"I do."

"Get it."

He unzipped his pack and pulled out what looked like parachute cord.

"Toss it over here. And put your hands behind your back," she said.

He did, not making eye contact. With a fortifying breath, she grabbed the rope off the ground and climbed over the downed tree.

"Lean forward."

He did as ordered. "I'm not going to hurt you."

"You're right, you won't."

She quickly bound his wrists behind his back, and secured him to a limb of the fallen tree. She stood and started walking.

"Drink some water," he said. "It will help with the headache."

"You can stop now."

"The best cell reception is over there, by that cluster of boulders." He nodded, ignoring her comment.

With determination and focus, she marched toward the field, on the other side of a narrow creek. That had to be the spot where she'd find a signal. It would also put her out in the open, making her vulnerable, an easy target. No, these guys usually worked alone. She checked his phone, hopeful and more than a little desperate, but she still had no bars.

She glanced up. A ray of sunlight bounced off the creek and pierced her vision. Pain seared through her brain. She snapped her eyes shut, but it was too late. A sudden migraine blinded her.

She stumbled forward. Had to get to…had to get service. Call her boss…

"What's wrong?" Will shouted.

She broke into a slow jog. Had to get away from him. Get help.

Breathing through the pain, she stepped onto the rocks to cross the creek. One foot in front of the other. She could do it.

But she slipped, jerking forward. She put out her hands to break her fall.

And landed in the water with a splash.

The man's shouts echoed in the distance.

She feared he would somehow free himself and finish her off.

She crawled through the creek, her soggy clothes weighing her down. Pain bounced through her head like a pinball.

With a gasp, she surrendered—to the pain, to her own failure—and collapsed into the cold, bubbling water.

TWO

"Ma'am!" Will shouted, pulling on the rope binding his wrists. She was down, unconscious in the creek. Was her head even above water?

"Hey!" He realized he didn't even know her name. "Ma'am, get up!"

She didn't move.

"Argh!" he groaned, pulling violently on his wrists. This was not going to happen. He was not going to sit here and watch a woman die in front of him.

"Get up!" he shouted.

She didn't move.

He yanked on his wrists and dug the heels of his boots into the ground, trying to get leverage. This craziness wasn't going to do him any good. He took a deep breath and forced himself to be calm.

"Think," he said. He remembered that his pocketknife was clipped to the side of his backpack.

He stretched out, making himself as long as possible, practically dislocating a shoulder in the process. With the toe of his boot, he caught the strap of his pack and dragged it across the soft earth. In a low crouch, he kicked it behind him until his fingers could reach the knife.

He flicked it open and sawed away at his bindings, unable to see what he was doing. A sharp pain made him hesitate when the blade cut his skin. He clenched his jaw and continued.

"Ma'am!" he called out. "Ma'am, answer me!"

She didn't move.

He continued to dig at the rope with the blade, and accidentally cut his skin again. Didn't matter, he had to get free and—

Snap! He jerked his wrists free, reached around and started working on the rope that bound him to the tree.

"Come on, come on," he muttered. The parachute cord he kept in his pack was meant to be strong, which was why it felt as if it was taking forever to cut himself loose.

Please, God, help me get to her in time.

He finally sliced through it, pocketed the knife and grabbed his pack. Racing across the property, he focused on the woman, who was only partially submerged in the creek. What if she'd swallowed water and it blocked her airway?

He rushed to her side, looped his forearms under her armpits and dragged her out of the creek.

He leaned close. She wasn't breathing.

"No," he whispered.

With one hand on her forehead, and the other on the tip of her chin, he tilted her head backward. He hoped it was only her tongue blocking the airway. He pinched her nose and administered two deep breaths.

She coughed and a rush of relief whipped through his chest. Will rolled her onto her side. "It's okay. You're okay now," he said, although his heart was still racing at breakneck speed.

He had to call for help, get Echo Mountain Search and Rescue up here and quick. He spotted his smartphone, partially submerged in the creek. He snatched it out of the cold water. It would dry out and be usable at some point, but until then Will was on his own.

The shiny glint of metal caught his eye. The woman's gun lay mere inches away from him. He wasn't a fan of guns, but couldn't leave it here for a random stranger to pick up. He shoved it into his pocket.

The woman coughed. "P-p-please don't hurt me."

He snapped his attention to her shivering body. She was clutching her jacket above her heart, terrified.

"You don't have to be afraid of me," he said. "I'm going to help you."

She closed her eyes, as if she didn't believe him. He wondered if she saw him pocket the gun and assumed the worst.

"Do you think you can get up?" he said.

"Yeah."

He extended his hand. She ignored it and shifted onto her hands and knees. A round of coughs burst from her chest. That didn't sound good. He feared the water in her lungs might lead to something worse.

She stood, but wavered. Her eyes rolled back and he caught her as she went down. Hoisting her over his shoulder, he marched to the cabin. He had to get her dry, tend to her head wound and then determine what other injuries she'd sustained. It was obvious she had a severe headache, and most likely suffered from dehydration. He could treat those easily enough, but didn't have the ability to treat internal bleeding from her fall, or other, more serious injuries.

He'd do his best. The rest was in God's hands.

Taking quick, steady steps, he made it to the cabin and laid her on the single bed. He grabbed logs and started a fire to warm the room. Once he got it lit, he refocused on the woman.

The woman. He wished he knew her name.

He pulled her into a sitting position, leaning her head against his shoulder to remove her jacket. He noticed it was water-resistant.

"Smart girl," he whispered.

Most of her clothes, except for her jeans, were dry thanks to the jacket. She could remove her jeans to dry out when she regained consciousness. He wouldn't do anything that would make her feel uncomfortable.

He adjusted her on the bed, covered her with a wool blanket and pulled the bed closer to the fire.

Rushing into the kitchen area, he grabbed more first-aid supplies from the cabinet. Her groan echoed across the small cabin. Cracking an ice pack a few times to release the chemicals, he grabbed a kitchen chair and slid it close to her.

"Let's get a better look." He analyzed the lacerations on her face, retrieved an antiseptic wipe from the first-aid kit, and pressed it against the scrapes scarring her adorable face.

Adorable, Will? Really?

Shaking off the thought, he cleansed the debris from her head wound, and then placed a bandage over the cut. He pressed the ice pack against a lump on her head that was sure to swell and probably leave her with at least one black eye, if not two.

"Uh," she groaned.

"I'm sorry, but this will reduce the inflammation."

She pinched her eyes shut as if in extreme pain, which indicated a concussion.

"Where else are you hurt?" he said.

She didn't answer. He noticed she gripped her left wrist against her stomach.

"Your wrist?" he said. "May I see it?"

She buried it deeper into her stomach. Yeah, it was injured, all right. Her reaction was similar to Marissa's when she'd broken her wrist after falling off her bike last spring.

The mystery woman wasn't making this easy, but he wouldn't force the issue. He suspected that dehydration intensified her confusion and fear, and he wouldn't risk making it worse.

He grabbed a water bottle out of his pack. "You need to hydrate."

Supporting her with his arm, he sat her up and offered the water. Slowly, her eyes blinked open.

"You really need to drink something," he encouraged.

She pursed her lips, and her blue eyes clouded with fear. Ah, she thought he'd put something in the water.

"It's filtered water, see?" He took a swig, and made sure to swallow so she could see him. "Delicious."

He sounded as though he was trying to convince five-year-old Marissa to eat her broccoli.

The woman nodded and he held the bottle to her lips. He tipped it and she sipped, but coughed. He pulled her against his chest and gently patted her back. How long had it been since he'd comforted a woman like this? Lord knew Megan wouldn't accept his comfort during the last months of her life.

The mystery woman leaned into Will and he held his breath. Maybe she'd decided to trust him?

"What's your name?" he said.

She pushed away from him.

He put up his hands. "I'm sorry."

Clutching her wrist to her stomach, her blue-gray eyes widened, her lower lip quivering.

"At least let me wrap your wrist?" he said.

She glared.

"The longer we wait, the more it will swell. I'll wrap it, then ice it to reduce the inflammation. It might hurt less once it's iced."

She didn't shake her head, so he thought she might be open to the idea. He pulled an elastic bandage out of his first-aid kit and extended his hand. "May I?"

She tentatively placed her wrist in his palm. It didn't look broken, but they wouldn't know for sure until she had it X-rayed.

"Did this happen when you fell in the creek?" he asked.

She nodded affirmative.

"It's probably a sprain." He slid his palm out from under her wrist. "I need you to hold this steady between your thumb and forefinger," he said, placing the bandage just right.

He wrapped the bandage down to her wrist and back up between her thumb and forefinger, noting how petite her fingers were.

"They'll obviously do this better at the hospital," he said, guiding the bandage to circle her wrist a few times. He secured it with a plastic clip. "I've got some pain reliever."

He dug in his backpack and found ibuprofen. When he turned to her, she'd scooted away from him again, her eyes flaring at the sight of the bottle.

"What do I need to do to convince you I'm a friend, not an enemy?"

"Give me my gun."

"I'd rather not."

She clenched her jaw.

"You're dehydrated and not thinking clearly," he explained. "The gun could go off by accident."

She pulled her knees to her chest, her hands trembling.

He grabbed an extra blanket off the foot of the bed and shook it open. He started to drape it across her shoulders, but noticed she'd gone white. He hesitated. Yet he had to get her warm somehow.

Gently draping the blanket around her, he pulled it closed in front.

"Hold it together," he said, as softly as possible.

She reached up with her right hand and their fingers touched.

She burst into a more violent round of shivers.

It tore Will apart that she was having this kind of reaction to him. Maybe it was a physical reaction to near hypothermia.

"We need to warm you up. Let me try something." He rubbed her arms through the thick blanket.

He thought he was being gentle, but after a minute she pinched her eyes shut as if suffering severe pain. He snapped his hands from her body and stood abruptly.

"You can't get warm with those wet jeans soaking your skin. You can take them off, and wrap this around your waist." He pulled his spare blanket out of his pack and laid it on the bed. "And ice the wrist. I'll go try to get the phone working."

He shifted his backpack onto his shoulders and turned to leave.

"Wait," she said.

He hesitated, hopeful.

"My gun?"

His heart sank. He pulled the weapon out of his jacket pocket and slid it onto the kitchen table.

"I'll be outside if you need me." Will shut the door and strode away from the cabin, kicking himself for his last remark. Of course she wouldn't need him. She thought Will the enemy, a man out to kill her.

"She's dehydrated," he muttered. "And confused."

Which made him a complete idiot for leaving her alone with the gun. Although he'd removed the clip, there was still one bullet in the chamber.

Talk about not thinking straight—he'd been thrown off-kilter since he'd found her. What else would explain his behavior? She'd practically broken his nose, yet he still wanted to help her. She'd tied him to a tree, and he'd cut his own skin to free himself so he could save her life.

He glanced at his wrist. He should have bandaged it while he was in the cabin, but had completely forgotten about his own wounds, and he'd left the first-aid kit behind. The cuts weren't that bad. A good thing since the woman would probably lock him out of the cabin.

The woman. He still didn't know her name.

He took the phone out of his pocket and removed the battery. Trying to power it up while wet could cause more problems, so he'd try to dry it out. He sat on a rock and dug into his pack for the small can of compressed air. His friends often teased him about the random things he carried in his pack, but after Marissa had dropped his phone into the town's water fountain, he knew anything could happen where his girls were concerned, and he had to be ready.

Glancing at the cabin, he realized he hadn't been ready for today's events. He hadn't been prepared to stumble upon a wounded, vulnerable woman in the mountains, nor had he been prepared to have to fight so hard to help her.

He aimed the compressed air nozzle at his phone and squeezed. As it blew away the moisture, he considered that maybe he should accept the fact he would never win this woman over. Perhaps he should cut his losses and head back to town, leaving her to her own devices until SAR could make the save.

He stilled, removing his finger from the compressed air button. No, he was not his father. He did not abandon those who needed him. Wasn't that exactly why he'd gotten involved in Echo Mountain SAR?

A crack of thunder drew his attention to the sky. Clouds rolled in quickly from the south. Not good.

Although the compressed air might have helped, he knew he'd have to wait a few hours before reinserting the battery and trying it out. He pocketed the phone and battery, and headed back to the cabin.

He hoped she wouldn't shoot him on sight.

As soon as he left, Sara grabbed the gun and sneaked out of the cabin. Maybe not the smartest move, but then staying with this man, this very manipulative man, could prove much worse.

She was actually starting to believe him.

As she trudged up a trail, clutching a wool blanket around her shoulders, she realized how close she'd come to dying back there at the hands of her captor.

Dying because he was so good at his job.

He'd nearly convinced her of his sincerity as he'd gently tended her wounds and warmed her body with his strong hands. And to think, when their fingers touched, she'd felt a sense of calm she'd never felt with another man.

Dehydration. A concussion. General insanity. Check on all of the above. LaRouche and Harrington must have paid big bucks to send such a master manipulator out here to find her.

At least she still had her gun. She pulled it out of her pocket, only then realizing the clip was missing. "Great."

Her head ached, her ribs ached and now her wrist was throbbing thanks to breaking her fall when she went face-down in the creek.

The creek. Will the assassin had saved her life after pulling her from the water. He hadn't had to do that, had he?

She focused on the rugged trail ahead to avoid any missteps. There'd be no one to catch her this time.

A flash of Will's green eyes assessing her injury as he'd held her upright taunted her. A part of her wished he'd truly been the man he'd claimed to be: a single dad on a hiking trip to commune with God.

But then, Sara wasn't a fool. She knew how *that* relationship worked—people prayed and God ignored them.

She stuck her gun back into the waistband of her wet jeans. At least she had one bullet left in the chamber.

A deep roar echoed through the woods. She froze.

Another roar rattled the trees.

She snapped her gaze to the right…

And spotted a black bear headed her way.

Everything in her body shut down—her mind, her legs, even her lungs. She couldn't breathe. Frozen in place, she stared at the beast as it lumbered toward her.

Closer.

Don't stand here, idiot. Run!

Could she outrun a bear? Were you even supposed to try? She struggled to remember what she'd learned about bears, but her brain had completely shut down. One thing she did know was that she couldn't defend herself if he decided she'd make a good appetizer.

"Don't run or he'll attack," a deep male voice said from behind her.

Will.

"Wh-wh-what are you…doing here?" she whispered, unable to take her eyes off the bear.

"Listen to me carefully. Do not look into the bear's eyes. Okay?"

She nodded and redirected her attention to the ground.

"Now back away slowly. Toward the sound of my voice."

She hesitated.

"It's okay. Slow movements shouldn't spook her," he said.

Sara followed his directions and backed up, but the bear kept coming. Will stepped in front of her.

The bear roared, aggravating her headache.

"What does she want?" she said.

"Probably the same thing you want. To be left alone. Maybe she's got cubs nearby."

"I have the gun."

"That'll only make her angry. Back up slowly."

She took a step back, then another.

"That's it," he said.

As she and Will tried to distance themselves, the bear slowly followed.

"This isn't working," Sara said, panic gripping her chest.

"Easy now. Don't make eye contact. You're doing great."

Sara continued to step back. "What if she charges us?"

"We make ourselves big and threatening. I have a feeling you'll do great."

Was he teasing her? As they were both about to be torn apart by a bear?

They kept backing away and Sara was stunned when the bear hesitated.

"That's right, we're boring hikers, mama bear," he said in a hushed voice.

That smooth, sweet voice he'd used on Sara.

They backed away until they were out of sight. Will turned and gripped her arm. "Let's move."

"You think she'll follow us?"

"Doubtful, but we're safer in the cabin. What were you thinking, taking off with nothing but a blanket?"

"I was… That you were—"

"Enough. I don't want to hear any more about how I'm going to kill you. The dehydration is messing with your head." He stopped and looked deeply into her eyes. "If I wanted you dead, I would have let Smokey eat you for dinner, right?"

True. An assassin wouldn't have risked his own life to save a mark from a bear, only to kill her later. In LaRouche's and Harrington's minds, a dead witness was the best witness, yet Will have saved her twice.

Which meant she'd been abusing this innocent man, Good Samaritan.

Single father.

She sighed as they kept walking.

"Thanks," she said. "For the bear thing."

"You're welcome. I don't suppose that warrants me knowing your name?"

"Sara."

"Nice to meet you, Sara. I'd rather you not run off again and get eaten by wild animals on my watch."

"No promises," she half joked.

"Ah, you like pushing back for the fun of it," he teased.

But he'd nailed it. Sara was always pushing, although, not necessarily for fun.

"Why do you think someone wants to harm you?" he asked.

"I witnessed a crime."

They turned a corner and he stopped short.

"What?" She looked around him.

A man was coming out of the cabin.

"Do you recognize him?" she said.

"No." He motioned to a nearby tree. "Hide back there. I'll check it out."

"It could be dangerous."

"Or simply a hiker lost in the mountains. Kinda like you." Will smiled and nodded toward the tree. "Go on."

"Maybe you should take this." She offered him the gun.

An odd smile creased his lips. “Thanks, but you keep it.”

She nodded and watched him walk away, shielding herself behind the tree. From this vantage point she could watch the scene unfold, not that she had a great escape plan. Hiking back up the trail meant crossing paths with the bear, but sticking around meant being interrogated by the real assassin, if that’s who the stranger was.

If it was the man hired by LaRouche and Harrington, that meant Will, a single father of two girls, was walking into trouble.

For Sara.

“No,” she whispered, and peered around the tree, wanting to go to him, to tell him not to take the chance.

A gunshot echoed across the property.

And Will dropped to the ground.

THREE

Will hit the dirt, thinking Sara had come after him and took her best shot. But that didn't make sense. She was smart enough to know it was safer where he'd left her, camouflaged by the trees.

Sara might be confused, but she wasn't foolish.

He struggled to slow the adrenaline rush flooding his body.

"Hey, sorry about that," a man's voice said.

Will eyed a man's hiking boots as he approached.

"I saw a mountain lion and wanted to scare him off."

Will stood and brushed himself off, irritated both by the hiker's decision to discharge a firearm and by his own reaction to the gunshot. It was a defense response developed from growing up in a house with a volatile, and sometimes mean, drunk.

"I'm B. J. Masters." B.J. extended his gloved hand and Will shook it.

"Will Rankin."

B.J. was in his late thirties, wearing a top-quality jacket and expensive hiking boots. He didn't seem like an amateur hiker, nor did he seem like the type to be hunting a helpless woman.

"Whoa, what happened?" B.J. motioned to Will's face.

Bruising must have formed from Sara nailing him with the gun.

"Embarrassing hiking moment," Will said. "Would rather not go into the details. I noticed you were in my cabin."

"Yeah, sorry about that," B.J. said, glancing at the ground.

"I thought maybe it was abandoned, but once I went inside I saw your things and the fire going. Didn't mean to trespass."

"No problem. You on a day hike or…?"

"Yeah, I'm scouting places to hold a retreat for guys at work. I'm with Zippster Technologies out of Seattle." He handed Will a business card. "I was surprised to see a cabin in this part of the park."

"A well-kept secret. Where are you headed today?"

"Squawk Point."

"That's a nice area," Will said.

He eyed Will's cabin. "You rent the cabin through the park website?"

"I do."

"I wonder how many guys could fit in there?"

"Probably eight to ten," Will said. "After that it might get a little crowded."

"Yeah, well, probably not big enough for our team." B.J. gazed across the field, then back at the cabin. "But a nice area, for sure. Well, thanks for not calling the cops on me for breaking and entering."

"Actually, I dropped my phone in the creek. Don't suppose I could borrow yours to call my girls and let them know I'm okay?"

Will figured he'd call SAR.

"Wish I could help you out, but the battery's dead. This new-model smartphone is worthless."

"What if you run into trouble?"

"I've got a personal locator beacon. Besides, what trouble could I possibly get into out here?" He gazed longingly at the mountain range.

"You'd be surprised," Will muttered.

"Well, nice meeting you." B.J. extended his hand again.

"You, too. Have a good day."

With a nod, B.J. headed for the trail.

Will went to the side of the cabin and pretended to get wood for the fireplace. Once B.J. was out of sight, he'd retrieve Sara and bring her to the cabin. Made no sense letting B.J. know of her presence, especially if the men who were after her questioned random hikers about seeing her.

When he'd found Sara just now, he noted her pale skin and bloodshot eyes. At least she was walking around, and maybe even thinking a little more clearly than before.

That woman was tough, no doubt about it, tough and distrusting.

Will wandered to the side of the property to search for a cell signal. The sooner he could get Sara medical attention the better.

He pressed the power button, but the phone was still dead.

He gazed off into the distance. B.J. was turning the corner, about to disappear from view. Will waited until he could no longer see the hiker, then started for the trail where he'd left Sara. She was already on her way down, clutching the gun in her right hand.

"Who was that?" she said.

"A techie from Seattle scouting out retreat spots."

"And you believed him?" She scanned the area.

"Sara, it's okay." He reached out.

His mistake.

She jerked back as if his touch would sear her skin. "Get inside."

He put up his hands and prayed for patience. What more could he do to make her feel safe?

"Are you hungry?" he said, going into the cabin. "I thought I'd heat up some red beans and rice for supper."

She followed him inside and shut the door. "I'm fine."

"I didn't ask if you were fine. I asked if you were hungry."

"Stop being nice to me."

"Would you rather I be mean to you?" He pulled out supplies for dinner.

"He could have been working for Harrington and LaRouche," she said.

"Doubtful. He gave me his business card." Will offered it to her. She took it and sat on the bed, still clutching the gun.

He pulled out a pot and found a can opener in a drawer. "As soon as the phone dries off, I'll get a signal and call SAR, but it might not be until tomorrow morning."

"Go ahead. Ask me," she said.

"Ask you what?"

"What I'm doing out here, and why men from a tour group I was assisting with are after me."

"My goal is to get you back to town for medical attention. If you want to tell me what's going on, that's completely up to you."

He heard the bed creak and her soft groan drift across the cabin. She was hurting. The adrenaline rush from her encounter with the bear had probably masked her pain, and now that she considered herself relatively safe, she was feeling every ache, every pinch of pain.

"How about some pain reliever?" he asked.

"Yeah, probably a good idea."

"Check my backpack, side pocket," he said, pleased that she was accepting his help. "You'll find a small container with ibuprofen and vitamins. Probably wouldn't hurt for you to chew on a few vitamin Cs to boost your immune system."

Filling the pot with water, he went to the fireplace to warm it. He didn't look at her for fear he'd scare her again, that she'd retreat behind a wall of paranoia and fear.

"Wouldn't hurt to drink more water," he suggested. "To help the dehydration, and probably the headache."

She grabbed the water bottle off the bed and sipped.

"Why are you here?" she said.

"It's my cabin, at least for a few more days."

"Why don't you leave me alone?"

"That wouldn't be very gentlemanly of me."

"Gentlemanly, huh?" she said.

"You sound as if you've never heard the word before." He stirred their dinner.

"Or I haven't met many—" she paused "—gentlemen."

"That's unfortunate."

"It's life."

He dropped the subject, not wanting to antagonize her with a philosophical discussion on how men were supposed to be gentlemen, especially to women, that men weren't supposed to think solely of themselves.

And abandon their children to a volatile mother.

Whoa, shelve it, Will. This getaway was supposed to be about easing the resentment from his heart, not battling the scars from childhood.

Out of the corner of his eye, Will noticed Sara shivering as she popped off the top of the ibuprofen bottle.

"If you remove your wet jeans we can dry them by the fire," he offered.

"No, thanks."

"Okay."

"No offense, but I won't get very far without my pants."

"Nor will you get very far if you come down with pneumonia."

"Okay, Dad."

He sighed. "Sorry, guess I clicked into parent mode."

He refocused on the water heating in the pot. For whatever reason, she still couldn't completely trust him.

Understanding comes from walking in the other person's shoes. Reverend Charles's advice when Will struggled to understand Megan. No matter how hard he'd tried, he couldn't make sense of why she'd pushed him away.

Since he and Sara would be stuck in this one-room cabin for a while, he tried seeing the world from her point of view to better understand her reactions. She seemed clearheaded, not as delusional as before, and she feared someone was out to harm her. That was her reality. He had to respect that fact. She was also wounded and stuck in a remote cabin with a stranger who, in her eyes, was somewhat of an enigma because he considered himself a gentleman.

The fact that the thought of a good man was so foreign to Sara probably intensified her distrust.

Will realized that in order to take care of her, he needed to respect her space, and not act aggressive or domineering. He hoped she would open her mind to the possibility that he truly wanted to help.

Gripping the gun firmly in her hand, Sara found herself struggling to stay awake. Not good. Things happened when she slept.

Bad things.

"Do you have any coffee?" she asked.

"Sure."

Will went into the kitchen. She eyed the bottle of ibuprofen in her lap, then the chewable vitamin C tablets. She'd taken both, thanks to Will's suggestion.

Will. A stranger with really bad timing who'd happened upon a woman with a target on her back. A stranger who wouldn't leave her, even after she'd told him her life was in danger, that she could be putting his life in danger.

"It's instant," he said, returning to the fire to warm water.

"That's fine." She handed him the chewable vitamin bottle. "You could probably use some extra C, as well."

He popped one into his mouth. "Thanks."

She watched his jaw work and his Adam's apple slide up and down as he swallowed. He fascinated her, this gentle, strong and honorable man.

He scooped coffee into a mug and added water. "You can take up to five of those vitamin Cs if you want."

"What I want is to be home," she let slip.

"Which is where?" He handed her the mug.

She noticed blood smudging his skin. "What happened to your wrist?"

"Ah, nothing," he muttered. He dug into his pack and pulled out an antiseptic wipe. "I'll bet you're a city girl."

"That obvious, huh?"

"A good guess."

"What about you?" she said.

"I live in Echo Mountain," he said as he cleaned blood from his wrist.

"What's that like, living in a small town?"

"It's nice, actually." He opened a dehydrated packet of food, poured hot water into it, sealed the bag and set it aside. "Never thought I'd end up living in a small town, but I've been here for ten years and can't imagine living anywhere else."

"You moved here from…?"

"Denver," he said. "My wife was from here originally, but she wanted to live near the Rockies so she got a job in Denver after college. We met on a group hike and…" He glanced at the fire.

"What?" Sara asked.

Will stood and went to the kitchen. "I should find us something to eat on."

She sensed he regretted talking about his wife. Sara wondered what had happened to her but wouldn't ask.

"Tell me more about your girls," she said.

Walking back to the fire, he handed her a spoon. She used it to stir the instant coffee.

"Claire's my eldest daughter. Eight going on eighteen." He shook his head and sat in a chair beside the fire. "I'm not sure how I'm going to make it through her teenage years without getting an ulcer."

"That's a ways away. Perhaps you'll remarry."

The flames danced in his green eyes as he stared at the fire. "Perhaps."

"How long were you married?" she pushed, sipping her coffee.

"Ten years. Claire was six when her mother died, and little Marissa was only three."

"It's hard for kids to lose a parent."

"So I've been told," he said.

There wasn't a day that went by that Sara didn't ache for her mom and dad.

She pulled the blanket tighter around her shoulders. They spent the next few minutes in silence. Will seemed temporarily lost in a memory about his wife, and Sara beat herself up for not getting enough evidence to put LaRouche and Harrington away sooner.

Sure she'd recorded their conversation and the murder, but when she'd checked her phone earlier, she'd noticed it had been damaged in the fall. Hopefully a tech could retrieve the file.

Will opened the packet of rice and beans, dumped it onto a metal plate and handed it to her.

"What about you?" she said.

"I'll eat whatever's left over."

She hesitated before taking it.

"Go on, it's not bad," he said.

"But it's your food."

"I've got more."

She took the plate, avoiding eye contact. The more time she spent with Will, the more frustrated she became about her situation, and relying on his good nature.

Relying on anyone but herself was dangerous.

Since she hadn't eaten in nearly eighteen hours, she took the plate. "Thanks."

"Tell me more about the man who is after you," he said.

"Hired by two businessmen who killed their partner." She took a few bites of food and sighed. "I saw them toss the guy over a cliff."

"They killed their partner?" he said. "Why?"

"Who knows, money?" She didn't want to share too much with Will because it could put him in danger.

"I can see why you've been so frightened," he said. "I'm sorry if I haven't been patient enough."

Her jaw practically dropped to the floor. What was he

talking about? He was apologizing after everything she'd done? Given him two black eyes and verbally abused him?

After a few minutes, she handed him the half-empty plate.

"You sure?" he said. "I can always heat up something else for myself."

"No, go ahead."

With a nod, he accepted the plate and started eating. She took a deep breath, then another, staring into the fire.

Maybe it was the flames dancing in the fireplace, or the sound of his spoon scraping against the plate. Whatever the case, she found herself relaxing, fighting to keep her eyes open.

Stay awake!

"Relax and I'll keep watch," he said, as if sensing her thoughts.

Will might think they were safe in the cabin, but Sara knew better. Danger was almost always on the other side of a closed door.

The warmth of the fire filled the cabin and she blinked, fighting to stay alert. Exhaustion took hold and she felt herself drift. She snapped her eyes open again, and spotted Will lying on the floor on top of his sleeping bag. He wore a headlamp and was reading a book.

He was definitely a trusting man, but was he really so naive to think they weren't in danger? He was a civilian determined to protect her. Yet she'd brought the danger to his doorstep.

For half a second, she wanted to believe there were quality men like Will Rankin who rescued failed FBI agents, and protected them from bears and assassins.

Comforted her with a gentle hand on her shoulder. She drifted again…

Don't make a sound...

She gasped and opened her eyes. Will was no longer on the floor beside the fire. She scanned the room. She was alone.

The door opened and she aimed the gun. Will paused in

the threshold. “Needed more wood.” He crossed the small cabin and stacked the wood beside the fireplace.

“What time is it?” she said.

“Nineish,” he said.

“I’ve been out for…”

“A couple of hours. Your body needed it.”

Her mind ran wild, panicked about what could have happened in the past two hours. How close the assassin was to finding her.

“Give me your phone.”

He handed it to her. She stood and headed for the door.

“I don’t think it will work yet,” he said.

“I’ve got to try.”

“Want me to come with?”

“No.” She spun around and instinctively pointed the gun at him. The look on his face was a mixture of disbelief and hurt.

“Sorry.” She lowered the gun. “Just…stay here.”

“Try a few hundred feet that way.” He pointed, and then turned back to the fire, his shoulders hunched.

The minute she stepped out of the cabin a chill rushed down her arms. She should have brought the blanket with her, but wasn’t thinking clearly. Why else would she have pointed the gun at Will?

His hurt expression shouldn’t bother her. She hardly knew the man. Yet shame settled low in her gut.

Focus! It was late, but she had to call her boss if she could get a signal.

The full moon illuminated the area around the cabin. She pressed the power button and practically jogged toward a cluster of trees up ahead.

“Come on, come on.” She held the button for a few seconds. The screen flashed onto the picture of the two redheaded girls.

“Yes,” she said.

But still, no signal.

She waved the phone above her head, eyeing the screen, looking for bars.

The click of a gun made her freeze.

"There you are."

FOUR

A firm hand gripped a fistful of Sara's hair. "Did you think you could outrun us?" a man's deep voice said.

Us? They'd sent more than one of them after her?

"Nice to meet you, Sara. I'm Bill." He snatched the gun from the waistband of her jeans and pushed her toward the cabin.

"What do you want?"

"Why'd you run off from the group?"

"I had a family emergency."

"Sure," he said, sarcastic. "Who sent you in the first place?"

"No one. I work for Whitman Mountain Adventures."

"Convenient how you showed up out of nowhere and worked your way onto LaRouche and Harrington's camping trip."

"I needed the job."

"Yeah, yeah. We're meeting up with them tomorrow so you can explain yourself. We'll sleep here tonight."

Sleep here? In the cabin? Where Will was innocently stoking a fire?

"No," she ground out.

"Yes." He shoved her forward.

She opened the door to the cabin, but Will was gone.

"Where's your friend?" the man asked.

"What friend?"

He pushed her down in a chair. "The guy I met earlier today. Before our pleasant chat, I noticed your torn jacket on the bed. I guessed you were close. Where'd he go?"

"I have no idea."

A thumping sound echoed from the front porch.

"You sit there and be quiet while I go hunting." Her attacker bound her wrists in front.

When she winced at the pressure against her sprained wrist he smiled as if taking pleasure in hurting her. He leaned close. So close she was tempted to head-butt him. Instead, she stared straight ahead, acting like the innocent victim she claimed to be. He tied another rope around her midsection, securing her to the chair.

"Behave," he threatened.

He turned and went outside in search of Will. Why had Will gotten himself involved in this? Why had he had to help her when he'd found her unconscious body next to the lake?

Silence rang in her ears as fear took hold. The assassin would kill Will, leaving two little girls without a father. No, she couldn't let that happen. Couldn't let those girls suffer through the kind of mind-numbing grief Sara had experienced, especially since Will's girls had already lost their mom.

"Never give up," she ground out. And she wouldn't, ever, unlike the cops who'd given up on finding Dad's killer.

She dragged the chair into the kitchen, awkwardly opening drawers in search of a weapon.

She found a multipurpose fork in a drawer. It would have to do.

The door swung open with a crash.

She spun around, aiming her weapon…

At Will.

"You're here," she gasped.

He rushed across the small cabin. "Are you okay? Did he hurt you?" Will untied her and searched her face, as if fearing she'd been beaten up.

Sara shook her head. "I'm sorry, I'm so sorry."

"It's not your fault." He led her back to the fireplace, removed his backpack and dug inside. "Let me find—"

The assailant charged into the cabin, wrapping his arm around Will's throat.

"Let him go!" she cried.

Will tried to elbow the guy in the ribs but the assassin was too strong. Digging his fingers into the guy's arm, Will gasped for air. Sara darted behind the guy and wrapped her arm around his neck. The guy slammed her back against the cabin wall, sending a shudder of pain through her body. She collapsed on the floor.

He dragged Will outside and Sara stumbled after them. "Stop! Let him go!"

He threw Will to the ground and stomped on his chest, over and over again. "You like that?"

"Leave him alone!" Sara charged the assassin. He flung her aside, but not before she ripped the gun from the waistband of his jeans.

He continued beating on Will, unaware she had his weapon.

Sara scrambled to her feet. Aimed the weapon. "Stop or I'll shoot!"

The assassin was drowning in his own adrenaline rush, the rush of beating a man to death. She squeezed the trigger twice and the guy went down. She rushed to Will, who'd rolled onto his side clutching his stomach.

"Will? Will, open your eyes."

He coughed and cracked them open. "That was…the guy who was after you?"

"He was hired to find me, yes."

"So someone else will come—" he coughed a few times "—looking for you?"

"Not tonight. He was supposed to take me to meet up with them tomorrow."

"Is he dead?"

"I don't know."

Will groaned as he sat up, gripping his ribs. "We need to check. If he's not dead, we need to administer first aid."

She leaned back and stared at him, stunned by his comment. "He tried to kill you."

He pressed his fingers to the assassin's throat. A moment later he nodded at Sara. "He's gone."

Will coughed a few times as he scanned the area. "We can't leave him out here. Animals."

She didn't have a response for that, either, speechless that Will could show compassion for a man who most certainly would have beaten him to death if she hadn't shot him first.

She eyed the body.

The dead body.

She'd just killed a man.

Her fingers tightened around the grip of the gun and her hand trembled uncontrollably, sending a wave of shivers across her body.

"Whoa, whoa, whoa," Will said, rushing to her. "Let's get you inside."

She thought she nodded, but couldn't be sure.

"Relax your fingers," he said, trying to take the gun away.

Staring at her hand, she struggled to follow his order but couldn't seem to let go.

"Sara, look at me."

She took a quick breath, then another. With a gentle hand, he tipped her chin to focus on his green eyes. Green like the forest after a heavy rain.

"That's it," he said. "Everything's okay. You can let go now."

But she didn't feel okay. Her hands grew ice cold and thoughts raced across her mind in a random flurry: her boss's disappointed frown, her cousin Pepper's acceptance into med school, the look on her father's face when he savored a piece of coconut cream pie.

A long time ago. Before…before…

Her legs felt as if they were melting into the soft earth.

She gasped for air…

And was floating, her eyes fixed on the moon above before she drifted into the cabin.

It was warm inside. It smelled like burning wood, not death. She was placed on the bed in front of the fire, but she didn't lie down because she didn't want to sleep, to dream, to be held captive by the nightmares.

"Keep the blanket around your shoulders," Will said.

It was then that she realized he'd carried her inside. He pulled the blanket snugly around her, and poked at the fire. It flared back to life.

He kneeled in front of her. "You're probably going into shock, but you'll be fine."

Those green eyes, brimming with promise and sincerity, made her believe that things would actually be okay.

It only lasted for a second.

Because in Sara's life, things were never okay.

"I'll be right back." Will squeezed her shoulder and left.

That was when the terror of her life came crashing down on her.

If she were a religious person, she'd go as far as to say she'd sinned in the worst possible way.

She'd killed a man.

She'd become like the monsters she'd sworn to destroy.

Like the monster that killed her father.

Will clicked into overdrive. He tossed logs out of the wood container, rolled the body onto a tarp and dragged him across the property.

A part of him was shocked, both by the murder of a stranger, and by his own reaction. He found himself more worried about Sara than the ramifications of this man's death.

It should be justified in the eyes of the law, since she'd shot him to save Will's life. The guy would have surely beaten Will to death, leaving his children parentless. Will wasn't sure Sara had had another option. The man was about brutality and death, and that was how his life had ended.

But taking another man's life was a sin, so after Will placed the body and weapon into the wood container, he kneeled beside it and prayed. "Father, please forgive us. In our efforts to live, we took another man's life."

Guilt clenched his heart. He still couldn't believe what had happened. But he couldn't dwell on it, not while Sara was going into shock. He needed to tend to her.

As he went back to the cabin, he noticed the man's blood on his gloves. He took them off and dropped them outside the door. The sight of blood might upset her further. He stepped inside the cabin.

Sara was not on the bed where he'd left her. He snapped his head around. "Sara?" His heart slammed against his chest. Had she left again? Was she wandering aimlessly in the mountains in a state of shock?

"Sara!"

The echo of his own voice rang in his ears. He turned, about to race out into the dark night.

Then he heard a squeak. Hesitating, he waited to see if he'd imagined it. Another squeak drifted across the room. He slowly turned back. The sound was coming from under the bed.

Will went to the bed and checked beneath it. Sara's terrified blue eyes stared back at him.

"He won't see me in here," she said in a childlike whisper.

"No, he won't. That's a good hiding place." He stretched out on his back and extended his hand. She looked at it. "Your hands must be very cold," he said.

She nodded. "Like ice-cycles."

"My hand is warm. May I warm the chill from your fingers?"

Her eyes darted nervously beyond him. "What if he comes back?"

"He won't. He's..." Will hesitated. Reminding her she'd

killed a man would not help her snap out of shock. "He's gone."

"Are you sure?"

"One hundred and ten percent." The number he used with his girls.

She eyed Will's hand. He motioned with his fingers to encourage her to come out.

"I'm only safe if I stay hidden," she whispered. "He won't see me in here."

That was the second time she used the phrase *in here.* Where did she think she was? Will suspected she might be drifting in and out of reality, the present reality mixed with a past trauma, perhaps? At any rate, he needed to keep an eye on her condition by making sure she was warm and comfortable. If she felt most comfortable under the bed, then that was where she'd stay.

"Are you warm enough?" he asked.

She shrugged.

"How about another blanket?" He snatched one off a chair and placed it on the floor.

Her trembling fingers reached out and pulled the blanket beneath the bed. "Thanks."

"Is there anything else I can do for you?" he said.

"No, thank you."

He positioned himself in front of the fire. A few minutes of silence passed as he stared into the flames. The adrenaline rush had certainly worn off, because he was feeling the aches and pains from the beating he'd survived.

Survived because of Sara. She'd saved him from an ugly, painful death.

As energy drained from his body, he struggled to stay alert. Will needed to protect Sara, take care of her.

He glanced left. Her hand was sticking out from beneath the bed. Was she trying to make a connection with him? He positioned himself on the floor and peered under the bed.

She'd changed positions and was lying on her side, bundled up in the blankets.

Bending his elbow, he brushed his hand against her petite fingers. She curled her chilled fingers around his.

"Wow, you are warm," she said.

"Yeah," he said, barely able to speak. This connection, the fact that touching Will comforted her, filled his chest with pride.

"Do you have a fever?" she said.

"Nah. The warm body temperature is a family thing. My girls run hot, too."

"Your girls." She closed her eyes and started to pull away.

Will clung to her hand. "No, don't. I…I need the connection."

She opened her eyes. "You do?"

"Yes."

"But I've been horrible to you. Accusing you of being an assassin, tying you up." Her eyes widened. "Oh, my God, that's why your wrists were bleeding. You had to cut yourself free."

She snatched her hand from his and rolled away.

Well, good news was she'd returned to reality and was no longer caught up in some trauma from her past. The bad news was she blamed herself for whatever pain Will had suffered.

He went to the other side of the bed. The fire didn't light this part of the room so he couldn't see her face, but he still tried to connect with her, there, in the dark.

"It's not your fault," he said. "You were terrified and confused, and most likely suffering from dehydration."

"I gave you a bloody nose."

"I startled you."

"You were trying to help me." She sighed. "I'm so ashamed."

"Why, because you were protecting yourself from men who wanted to harm you? You should be proud. You escaped. You survived."

"No, they were right. I don't belong out here."

"Where, in the mountains?"

She didn't answer him.

"Sara?"

She rolled over again and he went to the other side of the bed. He bit back a groan against the pain of bruised ribs as he stretched out on the floor next to her.

"Could you do me a favor and stay in one position so I don't have to get up and down again?" he teased.

"I'm sorry."

"It's not that bad. But the ribs are a little sore."

"I meant, I'm sorry for everything that's happened."

"Sara, it's not your fault."

"Yes, it really is."

Silence stretched between them, punctuated by the sound of the crackling fire. Will sensed there was more behind her words, but he wasn't going to challenge her. He tried another strategy.

"Thank you," he said.

"For what?"

"For saving my life out there."

"You saved mine first." She extended her hand again and he grasped it. Unfortunately it was still ice cold.

"Do you want to sit by the fire to warm up?" he offered.

"Maybe later."

He sensed she was still frightened and probably felt vulnerable. But the more he knew about her situation, the better he could help her.

"Are you up to talking about what's going on?" he asked.

"Sure."

"Men are after you because you witnessed a murder?"

"Yes. They want to know what I saw, and what I heard."

"Did you hear anything?"

"Yes."

He waited.

"I shouldn't involve you further," she said.

"How can I help you if I don't know what's going on?"

"I would never forgive myself if you, or your girls, were threatened because of your association with me," she said.

She was a strong, determined woman, and an honorable one, as well. He couldn't fault her for that.

She yawned and pulled the blanket tight around her shoulder. She hadn't coughed in the past few hours, so he felt hopeful she wouldn't come down with pneumonia.

"Perhaps we should sleep," he suggested. "To be fresh for tomorrow. We'll need to hike a bit to find a cell signal."

"Okay, sleep sounds…good." She yawned again.

Although he knew sleep would help him function tomorrow, he doubted he could relax enough to drift off. He decided to brainstorm the necessary steps to get them safely back to town.

As options whirled in his brain, exhaustion took hold, making his mind wander to other things like his girls, his latest work assignment, Megan's death and the gray cloud of grief that hung over his house for so many months afterward. Could he have done something differently to help his girls adjust? No, ruminating about the past wouldn't help him raise his girls with love and compassion.

Sara squeaked and squeezed his hand. She must have fallen asleep. Will focused on the feel of her cool skin clinging to him, and decided he'd been given another chance to help someone.

And he wasn't going to blow it this time.

When Sara awoke, it took her a minute to figure out where she was, and whose hand she clung to.

Will.

Embarrassed, she considered pulling abruptly away, but didn't. She wanted another moment of peace, and it felt so comforting to be holding on to him.

He slept on his back, breathing slow and steady. She envied him for such a peaceful sleep. Since childhood she'd struggled with nightmares that often left her feeling exhausted in the morning.

With a sigh, he blinked open his eyes as if he knew she was watching him. He turned his head toward her.

"Good morning," he said, his voice hoarse.

"Good morning."

"Did you sleep okay?"

It was then that she realized she hadn't been plagued by nightmares. "Yeah, actually, I did."

"Good." He eyed his watch. "It's eight. We must have needed the sleep." He stood and offered his hand.

"I'm good," she said.

"Want me to make coffee?"

"That would be great." Sara climbed out from beneath the bed and stretched. "Uhh," she moaned. Her body ached from her fingertips to her toes.

"Hey, easy there." He went to her, touching her arm to help her sit in the chair.

"I'm okay, just sore." She looked up into his eyes. "Coffee will make it better."

"You got it."

A sudden pounding on the door made her gasp.

FIVE

"Where's the gun?" Sara said, anxiety rolling through her stomach.

"Outside in the wood container."

The pounding continued.

Will grabbed a log from the woodpile by the fireplace and motioned for Sara to get behind him. But she was no weakling, and no matter what injuries she'd sustained, she wasn't going to let Will fight this battle for her. He'd done enough.

Ignoring the pain of her injured wrist, she also grabbed a log and got on the other side of the door. If someone broke it down, he was going to get an unpleasant welcome.

The muffled sound of men talking on the other side of the door echoed through the thick wood. There were more than one of them? Not good. How had they found the isolated cabin? Then again, Bill had found it easily enough.

Another knock made her squeeze the wood so tight a sliver edged its way into her forefinger.

"Will? Will, you in there?" a male voice called.

"Nate?" Will dropped the log and reached out for the door.

Sara darted in front of him.

"Nate's a friend of mine, a cop," Will said. "It's okay."

She didn't step out of his way. She trusted Will but didn't trust the situation. It was too much of a coincidence that Will's friend happened to be hiking nearby.

"Sara, it's okay," Will said, touching her shoulder. "Trust me."

Maybe it was his gentle tone, or the sincerity of his rich

green eyes that eased her worry. With a nod, she stepped aside, but didn't drop the log.

Will opened the door and shook his friend's hand. "Man, am I glad to see you."

Nate was tall, like Will, with broad shoulders and black hair. He wore a heavy jacket and gloves. An older gentleman with gray hair stood beside Nate.

"Hey, Harvey," Will greeted. "What are you guys doing up here?"

"Got a SAR call," Nate said. "We knew you were up here and figured you might be bored so we decided to swing by and pick you up." Nate studied Sara with a raised eyebrow. "Obviously, not bored."

The older man snickered.

"Right, sorry," Will said. "Nate, Harvey, this is Sara. Sara, Nate's a detective with Echo Mountain PD."

Sara placed the log on the floor and shook hands with the men. "Nice to meet you."

Nate redirected his attention to Will. "I didn't know you were dating anyone."

"Dating? Wait, no, not dating," Will said.

She thought he blushed, but couldn't be sure.

"We met when..." Will glanced at her.

"Will saved my life," she explained to Nate. "I witnessed a murder, and I'm on the run from men who are out to kill me because of what I saw."

Nate narrowed his eyes at her. "Direct, aren't you?"

"We've had a long night," Will said. "A guy tried to kill me and Sara shot him. The body's in the wood container."

"Wait, you killed a man?" Nate said.

"I had no choice," Sara answered.

"We've gotta get her to the hospital," Will redirected. "She's got an injured wrist, possible head trauma and who knows what else. We need to move fast before they send someone else after her."

"Can you hike?" Nate asked her.

"Hiking's not good for her concussion," Will said.

"Let her speak." Nate studied Sara.

"Not far, and not very fast, unfortunately," she admitted.

"I'll stay with you two for protection and call dispatch to send another team with a litter. Shouldn't take more than an hour since they're already on their way. Harvey, go ahead and help with this morning's rescue."

"You got it. It was nice to meet you, ma'am," Harvey said.

"You, too."

Sara instantly liked Harvey. He reminded her of what her father might have been like had he lived.

She went back into the cabin and sat at the kitchen table. Why did she have to think about Dad today? She didn't need that guilt and sadness dragging her down while trying to puzzle her way out of this dangerous situation.

"Sara?" Will said.

She absently looked at him.

He studied her with a concerned expression. "You okay?"

How could he possibly know that she'd gone to that dark place again?

"Yes, I just want to get out of the mountains and go home."

Will sat beside her, and Nate leaned against the kitchen counter. "And where is home?"

She sensed him clicking into cop mode and she could understand why. If someone was out to get Sara, innocent civilians could be at risk.

"Seattle, but I'd taken a temporary job with Whitman Mountain Adventures out of Spokane Valley," she said. "They needed extra help with groups they were taking up into the mountains."

"So you're a tour guide?"

"A cook, mostly." It had been a good cover considering she'd cooked for her dad and brother after her mom had died. She felt it wise to maintain her cover for now.

"How long have you been with Whitman Mountain Adventures?"

"Nate," Will interrupted. "Can't you do this later? She's been through a lot."

"So you said," Nate studied her. "You shot a man."

"Because he was beating me to death," Will interjected. He yanked his shirt up to expose his bruised torso.

Sara had to look away, but noticed Nate's expression harden.

"Give it a rest," Will said. "I'll go get water to make coffee." He grabbed a metal bucket and headed for the door. Will hesitated and turned to Sara. "You'll be okay?"

"Sure."

Will shot one more cautionary nod at Nate, then left.

"You cold?" Nate said, wandering to the fireplace.

"A bit."

Nate stacked some wood in the fireplace and shoved kindling beneath it. It was awfully quiet all of a sudden, and Sara realized she missed Will's grounding presence.

Whoa, not good. She'd have to separate from him completely once they made it back to town because somehow she'd grown dependent on him.

"Ya know, Will's had a tough couple of years," Nate said, his back to her as he started the fire.

"He told me."

Nate snapped around. "What did he tell you?"

"That his wife died, that he has two little girls."

Nate refocused on the fire. "Then, you can understand why residents of Echo Mountain are protective of him."

"Yes, that would make sense."

"Very protective."

"I understand. You have nothing to worry about from me. I plan to distance myself from Will as soon as we get off this mountain."

An hour later, Will finally took a deep breath as they were headed down the trail toward town. Sara was secured to the litter carried by two SAR volunteers, while a second team handled the recovery mission of the dead body in the wood container.

It turned out they'd had an abundance of SAR volunteers for this morning's call, so they'd sent half of them to the cabin for Sara. Will, Sara and Nate hadn't waited long for a team, which was good because the tension in the cabin had been palpable.

Will wasn't sure what had transpired between Sara and Nate while he was getting water, but she didn't say much after Will's return. She stretched out on the bed and rested until the team arrived. Will asked Nate what had happened, but instead of answering, Nate fired off questions, asking Will what he really knew about this stranger. He went as far as to caution Will to keep his distance.

When they arrived at the hospital, SAR friends hovered around Will, worried about his condition. Surrounded by the group, he felt the love of family, even though they weren't blood relations. Then he spotted Sara, all alone, being wheeled into the ER. Will started to follow her but Breanna McBride, a member of the SAR K9 unit, blocked him.

"What happened to your face?" She eyed his bruises. "I thought you were on vacation."

"I was, but I went hiking and found an unconscious, wounded woman."

"Then, you should have called for help, not played hero," Grace Longfellow, another K9 SAR member scolded as she approached.

"I appreciate the concern," Will said. "I'd better find a doctor and have my ribs looked at."

"Your ribs, what happened to your ribs?" Breanna asked.

"And who gave you the black eyes?" Grace pushed.

"Ladies, I need to speak with Will," Nate interrupted, walking up to them.

"You can't. He has to see the doctor," Grace said.

"I'll make sure he does." Nate led Will away from Breanna and Grace.

"Thanks for the save," Will said.

"You're welcome, but I really do need to talk to you."

Will strained to see the ER examining room door. "I'd like to know how Sara's doing."

"Take care of yourself first."

"But—"

"Get looked at by a doctor. Then if Sara's story checks out, you can see her." Nate stopped and looked at Will. "Although, if someone's after her, wouldn't it be better to keep your distance?"

"But you're going to protect her, right?"

"We need to get all the facts."

"You don't believe that she's in trouble? Who do you think that guy was that she shot and killed? He would have killed her after he finished me off."

Nate planted his hands on his hips and sighed.

"What's wrong with you?" Will said, realizing his accusatory tone bordered on rudeness.

"I guess I'm a little more cautious than most," Nate said. "I don't necessarily believe people until I have proof. A man is dead—this is serious."

"You don't have to tell me that. Wait, are you thinking about arresting Sara? You can't. It was self-defense."

"I understand that, Will, but I still have to question her as soon as possible."

"I get it, but make no mistake that she's in danger. And she's all alone."

Nate put his hand on Will's shoulder. "Once they fix her up, I'll question her, confirm her story and we'll go from there, okay?"

Will nodded, but he wasn't totally satisfied. He didn't like the way Nate was talking about Sara, as if she was the suspect, not the victim.

"You'll see a doctor?" Nate said.

"Sure."

Nate nodded that he was going to stand there and watch

to make sure. With a sigh, Will went to the registration desk, described his injuries and was told to sit in the waiting area. He found a corner spot, away from people.

He closed his eyes and pressed his fingers to the bridge of his nose, needing to think, to pray. For Sara.

Please, God, keep her safe in your loving embrace.

“Am I intruding?” Breanna said.

Will opened his eyes. “No, but I'm not very good company right now.”

She sat down next to him. “You look worried.”

“I am.”

“About that woman? The woman you met yesterday?”

“Stupid, huh?”

She glanced sideways at him. “Hey, are you calling me stupid?”

“What? No, I—”

“I'm the one who rescued a semiconscious man from the mountains, remember?”

Will cracked a half smile. “Oh, yeah, forgot about that.”

“Then, you're the only one. My family still hasn't let me live that down.”

“But they like Scott. We all like Scott.”

“Not at the beginning they didn't. I rescued a wounded man with amnesia, who couldn't remember why men were shooting at him, and he had an unregistered gun in his hotel room. They thought I'd lost my mind.”

“I have a feeling Nate shares that same opinion about me.”

“Well, he didn't find her, did he? He didn't look into her eyes.”

“Or comfort her,” Will let slip.

“Or comfort her.” Breanna leaned toward him. “Don't let anyone make you feel ashamed about that, okay?”

He nodded.

“William Rankin?” a nurse called.

“That's me.” Will stood and nodded at his friend. “Thanks, Bree.”

“Anytime.”

* * *

The headache was the worst part of her physical injuries. Sara could tolerate pain from the sprained wrist and various aches whenever she moved, but the headache was nearly paralyzing.

Detective Nate Walsh's questions didn't help matters. His voice was starting to wear on her. She'd learned he'd been promoted to detective just last year, so he was probably trying to make a good impression on his superiors.

He was only doing his job by conducting his interview as soon as possible, but right now she was desperate to turn off the lights and sleep.

"So, Miss Long, you witnessed two men from your tour group, Mr. LaRouche and Mr. Harrington, throw a third man, Mr. Price, off the mountain. Why would they do that?"

"I don't know." It was the best she could come up with considering she wasn't ready to expose herself as an FBI agent, make that a rogue FBI agent on leave, which complicated things even more.

"You must have overheard something..."

Oh, she had. She'd heard LaRouche and Harrington try to convince David Price to get on board with their plan.

A criminal plan to distribute the dangerous drug Abreivtas into the United States.

"Sara?" the detective pushed.

"I'm sorry, what was the question?"

"What did you hear before they supposedly pushed Mr. Price over the edge?"

Supposedly. Right. The detective didn't believe her.

"They were arguing about a business decision, I think. David said he was done and started to walk away. Mr. LaRouche grabbed him and..." She hesitated. "Hurled him over the edge."

"And Mr. Harrington did nothing?"

"No, sir. I think he might have been in shock."

"Then what?"

"They heard me and turned around…"

The memory shot adrenaline through her body as she recalled the predatory look on LaRouche's face.

"Did Mr. LaRouche say anything?" the detective asked.

"No, sir. But he looked—" she hesitated "—furious. So I ran."

"Is it possible they got into an argument and the fall was an accident?"

She eyed the detective. Was he on LaRouche and Harrington's payroll? No, that couldn't be possible. Nate seemed like a solid guy and he was Will's friend, which went a long way in her book.

Will. A man you barely know. Maybe she didn't know him all that well, but she trusted him. Will was what her father used to call "good people."

"Ma'am?" Nate said. "Could the fall have been an accident?"

"No, I don't think so." She studied her fingers interlaced in her lap.

"Okay, so you took off and left your gear behind?"

"Yes, sir."

"Did they chase you?"

"Yes. I tried to escape down the side of the mountain and fell. Will found me the next day."

"And the man who attacked you and Will? Did you know him?"

"No, sir."

"Then, how did you know he was an enemy?"

"The way he yanked on my hair and threatened me."

"What did he say specifically?"

"He said, did I really think I could outrun them, and that he was ordered to bring me to a meeting the next day so I could explain myself."

"And then?"

"He tied me up and went to find Will. They fought—the

man was kicking Will to death, so I shot him." She eyed the detective. "Wouldn't you have done the same?"

Someone tapped at the hospital room door.

"Hey, Sara," Will said, joining them.

He went to the opposite side of the bed and gently placed his hand over hers. Although she sensed the gesture might be inappropriate in Nate's eyes, the contact instantly calmed her.

"How are you feeling?" Will asked, ignoring Nate, and searching her eyes.

"I'm okay. My head hurts, though."

"Want to buzz the nurse for a pain reliever?"

"No, I've already taken something. It should kick in soon."

Nate cleared his throat and raised an eyebrow at Will's hand, gently covering Sara's. She started to pull away, but Will wouldn't let her go. It wasn't a forceful grip; it was a comforting one.

Will looked at Nate. "I think she needs to rest."

"Is that right, Dr. Rankin?"

"She's not going anywhere. Can't you wait until she's feeling better to finish your interview?"

Nate directed his attention to Sara. "We're pretty much done, although I'd prefer you stay in town until we wrap this up."

"Of course," she said.

Nate directed his attention to Will. "I'll need to take your official statement, as well."

"I can swing by the station this afternoon."

"No, now. You can start with how you got the black eyes," Nate said.

"That was my fault," Sara said.

"A misunderstanding," Will offered.

"*She* gave you the black eyes?" Nate said.

"It was an accident," Will defended.

Nate raised an eyebrow.

"When I found Sara, she was unconscious," Will explained. "She regained consciousness and she thought I was one of the guys trying to hurt her. In an effort to defend herself, she nailed me with her weapon."

Sara didn't miss Nate's speculative frown.

"Continue," Nate said.

"I took her back to the cabin to tend to her injuries."

She appreciated that he didn't describe how horrible she'd been to him, verbally abusive and threatening, making snide remarks when all he wanted to do was help her.

"Last night she went outside to find a cell signal and I went to get more wood. I saw a man approach Sara from behind and force her into the cabin at gunpoint. I recognized him as a man I'd met earlier in the day. He seemed so innocuous. I've got bad instincts, I guess."

"Sociopaths can be charmers," Sara muttered, realizing the drugs might be loosening her lips a little too much.

"You saw him take Sara into the cabin. Then what?" Nate prompted.

"I tried luring him outside."

"Even though he had a gun and you didn't," Nate said disapprovingly.

Will seemed to ignore the tone of Nate's voice and continued, "He came outside, I knocked him out with a piece of wood and went to check on Sara," Will said. "I guess I didn't hit him hard enough because he came after me in the cabin, dragged me outside and kicked me until I nearly passed out. I heard two shots and he stopped kicking."

"As I said before in my statement, I shot him because I feared for Will's life, and my own," Sara added.

"You shot him with *your* gun?"

"No, the attacker's gun. I grabbed it when he was beating up Will and I was trying to pull him off."

"You shot him in self-defense?" Nate asked Sara.

"Yes."

"Then I put the body in the wood bin to keep it away

from animals," Will said, directing the detective's attention away from Sara.

"Why didn't you call for help?" Nate asked Will.

"I couldn't get a signal at the cabin, and I didn't want to leave Sara alone in search of one. She was exhibiting symptoms of shock. I'd hoped she'd be better by morning, at which time we'd hike a short distance to find a signal. Then you showed up."

"We'll have the deceased fingerprinted, which might give us some answers. That is, if he's even in the system."

"Oh, he will be," Sara said, her cop instinct stating the obvious.

"You sound pretty sure," Nate said. "Had you ever met him before?"

"No, sir, but I know his type."

"What type is that?"

Nate and Will looked at her, expectant. Oh, boy. She'd better come up with a good answer.

"Bullies," she said. "They're usually not one-time offenders, are they, detective?"

He hesitated, as if puzzling over her answer. "No, they're not."

Sara closed her eyes, hoping the detective would take the hint and leave. She needed time alone, without doctors and medical staff poking at her, and without the local police's pointed questions.

"Sara, have you ever shot a man before?" Nate asked.

She snapped her eyes open. "Of course not."

It was the truth. In her tenure with the FBI, she'd never found herself in a situation where she had to shoot and kill someone.

Until last night.

In order to save Will's life.

He was only in danger because of you.

"If you don't mind, I could really use some sleep." She rolled onto her side away from Nate and slipped her fingers out from under Will's hand. The guilt of putting him in harm's way weighed heavy on her heart.

"Will, you and I can finish your interview in the lounge."

"Okay," Will said. "Sara, I'll be close if you need me."

She had to distance herself from this man before he was even more seriously hurt because of Sara and her quest to nail LaRouche and Harrington. More seriously hurt? He was almost killed last night. The bruising below his eyes and swollen nose made her stomach burn with regret.

"No, you can leave," she said.

"Excuse me?"

"Just go, Will. You've done your bit."

"My bit?"

She mustered as much false bitterness as possible in order to drive him away. "Yeah, saving the damsel in distress. You're relieved of your duties."

She closed her eyes, hypersensitive to the sounds in the room: the clicking of the blood pressure machine, a car horn echoing through the window…

Will's deep sigh as he hovered beside her bed.

She'd hurt him with her acerbic comment, but it was for his own good. So why did she feel like such a jerk about the silence that stretched between them?

"Come on," Nate said.

She felt Will brush his hand across her arm—a good-bye touch.

A ball of emotion rose in her throat. This shouldn't hurt; she shouldn't feel anything for a man she'd only met yesterday.

Her emotional pain was a side effect of her injuries, that was all, the trauma of the past twenty-four hours. It had nothing to do with Will and his gentle nature, or his caring green eyes. She sighed, and drifted to sleep.

Sara awakened with a start.

Where was she? She sat up in bed and searched her surroundings. Right, she was in the hospital. It was dark outside; dark in her room. Someone had turned off the lights, probably to help her sleep.

"You're okay," she whispered.

But then why was her heart pounding against her chest?

She flopped back on the bed, remembering the nightmare that had awakened her—running down the middle of a deserted street, LaRouche and Harrington chasing her in a black limousine. Even as she slept, the corrupt businessmen were terrorizing her.

The intensity of her nightmare drove home how much danger she was in—even here, in a hospital. She was a target and she would continue to be a target until she put them behind bars.

Holding onto her IV pole, she went to the closet and found her now dry jeans. Although she favored her sprained wrist, she dressed herself, remembering how Will had offered to dry her jeans by the fire.

How he'd taken care of her.

Talk about a weak moment. After the shooting, she'd completely fallen apart, sucked into the black emotional hole of her past, remembering the sound of her father fighting for his life downstairs.

The sound of the gunshot that had taken his life.

If Will hadn't been there last night to talk her down from her traumatic shock, to offer her a blanket and a warm hand to hold on to, she would have spun herself into a blinding panic attack.

"You can't keep relying on him," she reminded herself. "You've got to do this on your own."

On her own. By herself. That had been Sara's mantra since childhood, even after her aunt and uncle had taken her into their home.

Today was no different. She had to protect herself, call in and update SSA Bonner about what had happened. He was going to be furious that she'd pursued this case against his orders, and she might even lose her job.

She hesitated and gripped the IV pole. Maybe she should wait to contact him until after she retrieved the recorded argument between the men—proof that there was truth to her claims about LHP, Inc.

Unless she had firm evidence in the death of David Price, it would be her word against LaRouche's and Harrington's. The word of two slick businessmen against Sara's, a rogue FBI agent with a chip on her shoulder who couldn't follow orders and took extreme measures to prove her point.

Maybe she should have dropped this case months ago and kept her mouth shut instead of hounding Bonner. But she couldn't watch the corporate hacks at LHP, Inc., get away with introducing a dangerous drug into the United States and promoting it as a safe and effective sleep aid. She'd uncovered solid evidence, buried reports from the pharmaceutical testing, even if Bonner thought them innocuous. She knew what Abreivtas could really do.

It could kill. She had to stop them.

She went into the bathroom and splashed water on her face. It wouldn't look good to local authorities if she left the hospital, but staying here made her a target. Detective Walsh didn't seem to be taking her story seriously, and even if he did, the local cops couldn't protect her from the likes of LaRouche's and Harrington's hired goons.

Drying her face with a paper towel, the image of Will being kicked, over and over again, flashed across her thoughts. She hated that she'd been responsible for such a violent act on a gentle man.

A widower and single parent. Hadn't he suffered enough?

Slipping into her jacket, she felt for her wallet and phone. They were both tucked into her inside zippered pocket. Good. She took a deep breath and pulled the IV out of her hand.

She peeked around the corner. All clear. She was far

enough away from the nurse's station that they wouldn't see her leave, and even if they did, they couldn't stop her, right?

She hurried to the elevator, but decided it was too risky. She didn't want to take the chance Nate Walsh had come back with more questions or, more likely, Will had returned to check on her.

She ducked into the stairwell and headed down. Gripping the handrail, she took her time. No need to rush and pass out before she got safely away.

Her head ached from the emotional tension and physical movement. She focused on taking slow and steady breaths.

A door opened and clicked shut from a floor above.

She hesitated.

"Sa-ra?" a man called in a singsong voice.

Her blood ran cold.

"I need to talk to you," he said.

She stumbled down the last few steps, tripping and slamming into the door to the first level. Whipping it open, she shuffled away from the stairwell. Eyes downcast, she wandered through the ER waiting area toward the exit.

And spotted a tall, broad-shouldered man coming into the hospital and heading toward her.

Don't be paranoid.

In his midthirties, he wore jeans, a fatigue jacket and military-grade boots.

Their eyes locked.

"Sara?" he said, reaching into his jacket.

She spun around and took off.

SIX

Will wasn't sure why he'd returned to the hospital. Sara had been pretty clear that she didn't want him around.

But something felt off. Her voice said one thing, but he read something else in her eyes. It was almost as if she thought sending him away was the right thing to do, yet she desperately wanted him to stay.

"Or you're losing it," he muttered as he parked the car.

At any rate, he'd decided to check on her. Maybe she'd be asleep, which would be the best scenario. He needed to see her and know she was safe, then he could leave.

Yeah, who was he kidding?

"What are you doing here?" Nate said from a few cars away. Apparently he'd had a similar thought, only a different motivation.

"Don't bust my chops," Will said. "I want to make sure she's okay."

"She's fine."

"I'd like to see for myself." Will continued toward the hospital entrance.

"Do I have to get a restraining order against you?"

Will snapped his attention to Nate. The cop's wry smile indicated he was teasing.

"Sara and I have been through a lot," Will said. "And last night..." He shook his head.

"Last night, what?" Nate challenged.

"I know it's your job to be suspicious, especially because she shot a man, but trust me, it was not something she enjoyed doing. She was traumatized afterward."

"She's not your responsibility."

"I didn't say she was."

"But you're coming here at—" Nate checked his watch "—nine fifteen to check on her?"

They entered the hospital and went to the elevators. "I've got nothing better to do. The girls are spending another night with their grandparents."

"Uh-huh."

"Hey, don't give me a hard time for being a good guy."

"Good guys finish last, remember?"

"I didn't know it was a race," Will countered.

"Just…be careful."

Will nodded his appreciation for his friend's concern. A lot of folks in town seemed concerned about Will since Megan had died. Did they all think him that fragile? Or incapable of making good choices?

As Nate and Will stepped out of the elevator onto Sara's floor, a frantic-looking officer named Spike Duggins rushed up to them.

"I went to grab a coffee," Spike said. "She was sound asleep. The nurse was going to keep an eye out."

A chill arced across Will's shoulders. "Sara's gone?"

"I notified security," Spike said, directing his answer to Nate.

"How long?" Nate said.

"I don't know, five, ten minutes?"

"You had her under surveillance?" Will asked Nate.

"Spike, you start at the north end," Nate said, ignoring Will's question.

"Spike, this is security, over," a voice on Spike's radio interrupted. "I think I spotted her in the lobby."

Nate grabbed Spike's radio. "Keep her there."

"She's already gone. I must have scared her off."

"Which direction?" Nate asked.

"Toward the cafeteria," the security officer said.

"Head to the south exit," Nate ordered him. "Spike will go north and I'll check out the cafeteria."

"Roger that," the security officer responded.

"What about—"

"You stay here in case she returns," Nate ordered Will.

The two men jogged off and disappeared into the stairwell.

Will couldn't stand here and do nothing. The security guard said he'd scared her off, so what made Nate think he and Spike would have better luck?

Was she having another flashback, like the one she'd had last night? If so, she wouldn't trust a stranger, or even a cop.

But she'd trust Will.

He went into her room and checked the closet. Everything was gone. She definitely hadn't planned to come back.

He took the stairs closest to the cafeteria and headed down.

Will had to find her, had to make her feel safe so she wouldn't run away. Perhaps if Nate had told her he'd left a police officer to guard her, she wouldn't have felt so vulnerable.

But Will sensed Nate's motivation had been to keep her under surveillance, not protect her from a violent offender. Will never should have left the hospital, even after she'd asked him to.

What was the matter with him? Why did he feel such a deep need to protect this woman?

Because of the look in her eyes and the sound of her voice when she'd hidden under the bed. He'd seen that look before on his sister's face when they'd hid from their raging mother. Will had perfected the role of protector at an early age.

He got to the ground floor and headed to the cafeteria, readying himself for the lecture he'd surely get from Nate. Will entered the empty dining area as Nate stormed out of the kitchen.

"I told you to stay upstairs," he snapped.

"She's frightened and she trusts me."

"Whatever. I'm going to check the security feed." Nate continued down the hall. "Go home, Will," he called over his shoulder. "You don't belong here."

Nate disappeared around the corner. His words stung, but only for a moment. Will knew Nate's comment was born of concern for Will.

As Will scanned the cafeteria, he considered the extent of Sara's injuries. She had winced if she moved too quickly, or put pressure on her wrist by accident. A woman in that kind of pain couldn't run for long. More likely she would hide until she saw an opportunity to quietly slip away.

He wandered through the cafeteria. The tables were empty, but a few visitors were standing at the coffee station filling up, probably in anticipation of a long wait ahead of them tonight.

His gaze drifted to a cluster of office plants in the opposite corner of the cafeteria, and he remembered what she'd said last night.

He won't see me in here.

Hiding meant safety to Sara. He approached the plants, fearing he was wrong and she wouldn't be there, in which case, she might be wandering the property somewhere, completely vulnerable. He clenched his jaw, fighting back his worry.

As he got closer, he saw the reflection of a woman hugging her knees to her chest against the glass window. With a relieved sigh, he devised a plan to ease her out of hiding. He wanted this to be her idea; he wanted Sara to feel in control.

He went to the hot drink station and plopped teabags into two cups, poured hot water and gave the cashier a few singles. He carried the hot beverages across the cafeteria and sat down near the plants.

"Sara, it's Will," he said. "I thought you might still be cold." He slid a cup toward her.

She didn't take it.

"Sorry it couldn't be something better, like a scone or a muffin, but food service pretty much shuts down at this time of night. That's herbal tea. It's orange blossom," he said. "The girls like that one, and I like it because it's caffeine-free and won't keep them awake."

"You shouldn't be here."

"I came back to check on you."

"No, you really shouldn't be here. It's dangerous."

"What do you mean?"

"I heard a man behind me in the stairwell. He said my name—they sent him to get me. I ran, and another man was blocking the exit."

"I think that was actually a hospital security officer."

"No, he was wearing military-grade boots. He also knew my name and was…was…"

"It's okay. You're safe now, and I'm not leaving until you believe that."

She reached out and took the cup. At least her fingers weren't trembling like they had been last night.

"How did you know I'd be here, behind the plants?" she asked.

"It seemed like a logical spot to hide out." He finally glanced at her. She looked tired, worn down and still frightened. "Did the man threaten you?"

"He said he needed to talk to me."

"But nothing else?"

"No, why? You think I'm crazy, too?" she snapped.

"Sara." He hesitated. "I'm on your side, remember?"

She tipped her head back against the glass and sighed.

"Here's a thought—why don't you work *with* the police instead of shutting them out?" Will said. "Detective Walsh can protect you."

"Detective Walsh doesn't even believe me."

"Don't be put off by his tone. He's a big-city detective turned small-town cop. He's got an edge to his voice, sure, but you want a tough guy like that on your side, don't you?"

"What I want is to get out of here, without putting anyone else in danger."

"Let me call Nate and have him escort you back to your room."

"Where I'm a sitting duck."

"Not if he offers twenty-four-hour police protection." He wasn't about to say that he would also stay close, because he knew she'd fight him on that decision.

"Okay, I guess that's the best choice, if you can get him to believe me."

"I'll talk to Nate. If he doesn't believe you, I'll talk to the chief. I've got some pull in this town."

"Yeah, I noticed how everyone surrounded you when we first arrived at the hospital. You have a great support system."

"I am blessed. For sure." He remembered how friends from church and SAR had rallied around him after Megan's death. How they wouldn't let him wallow, brought him meals and offered to entertain the girls.

But that was two years ago. He'd mostly healed and was a strong man, and a good father, even if his in-laws didn't always think so. Sure he'd stumbled a few times along the way, but today Will felt confident in his abilities to raise his girls with love and compassion.

"Okay, let's head back to my room," Sara said.

Will stood and offered his hand.

"Can you hold my tea?" she said.

"Of course." He'd wanted to take her hand, but would not force the issue. Taking her cup, he restrained himself as he watched her stand. It was frustrating to see her struggle against the pain. He tossed his cup into the garbage can behind him, and reached for her again.

"No, I can do it," she said.

He should respect her determination, not be hurt by it. The rejection wasn't a criticism of his abilities, but he sensed her need to rely on herself.

She straightened. “Thanks.” She stepped out from behind the plants and started across the cafeteria.

Will noticed a slight waver in her step and he reached out to steady her. His hand gripped her upper arm, and she snapped her gaze to meet his.

“It’s okay to accept help,” he said. “I won’t expect anything in return, promise.” He smiled, hoping to lighten the moment.

“No, you wouldn’t, would you?” she said in a soft, almost hushed voice.

For a moment, he couldn’t breathe. It was as if she saw right through him, into his wounded heart.

“We found her, sir,” a man’s voice said.

Sara ripped her attention from Will and paled at the sight of a man heading toward them. He was in his thirties, wearing jeans and a fatigue jacket. Will assumed it was the security guard, since he held a radio in his hand. Then Will noticed his boots—military grade.

“Are you the security officer?” Will clarified, to ease Sara’s worry.

“Yes, sir, Jim Banks, hospital security. Are you taking her back to her room?”

“I am,” Will said.

“Why aren’t you wearing a security uniform?” Sara pointedly asked.

“I’d already changed into street clothes when I heard the call go out that you were missing, so I thought I’d help find you before I left,” Jim said. “I’m sorry if I frightened you.”

She nodded, but didn’t look convinced.

“I’ll accompany you both to her room,” Jim said.

“Thanks,” Will said.

Sara didn’t look happy. For whatever reason, the security officer intimidated her. Will wasn’t sure why. The guy seemed okay to Will, but then Will hadn’t been the best judge of character or he would have figured out the friendly hiker from yesterday was really a hired thug.

They walked in silence to the elevator. As the doors opened, Nate came rushing around the corner.

"Someone was after her, here in the hospital," Will blurted out.

Nate nodded at Jim. "Thanks, I've got this."

Jim hesitated for a second, then with a nod, he said, "Have a good night."

"You, too," Will offered.

Will, Nate and Sara got into the elevator. Nate pressed the third-floor button. Sara leaned against the elevator wall, and Will shifted himself between her and Nate. It was an instinctive, protective gesture.

"When you disappear like that it makes you look as if you're hiding something," Nate said, eyeing the elevator floor numbers.

Sara didn't answer at first. Will knew if he answered for her, Nate would only criticize him and come down harder on Sara. She needed to explain her actions.

Will squeezed her hand and nodded, encouraging her to respond.

"I'm sorry. I was scared," she said. "I had a nightmare that reminded me how much danger I was in. I freaked out and took off, and some guy was stalking me."

"What did he say?" Nate said.

"That he needed to talk."

"Did you recognize him?"

"I didn't see him. I heard him."

"Where did this happen?"

"The stairs at the end of my hallway."

Nate sighed. "I'll post a uniform outside your room."

Will squeezed her hand.

"Thanks," she said.

They reached her floor. Will and Nate escorted Sara to her room, where Spike waited.

"I'm so sorry, ma'am," Spike said. "I stepped away for a minute and—"

"Officer Duggins will be relieved by Officer Pete Franklin in about half an hour," Nate said, narrowing his eyes at the young cop. "I'll also hang around for a while."

"No one's going to hurt you here," Will said, looking at Nate for confirmation. "Right?"

Nate nodded.

"Thanks." She glanced at Will as if she was going to say something. Instead, she offered a grateful smile, turned and went into her room.

Nate narrowed his eyes at Will. "I'll be here and Pete will show up soon."

"I'm still here," Spike offered.

"Don't push it," Nate warned, and then looked at Will. "You can really go now."

"I know." Will didn't move.

"But you're not going anywhere, are you?"

Will shrugged.

The next day Sara convinced doctors that her minor concussion and sprained wrist didn't warrant her staying in the hospital any longer, although once they released her she wasn't sure where she'd go. Nate had requested she stay in town until they finished their investigation of David Price's death.

There was still no word from LaRouche and Harrington. She wondered how they'd talk their way out of this one.

It didn't matter. At this moment what mattered was finding a safe place to stay, a place where her mystery stalker wouldn't torment her further.

She put on her torn jacket and left her hospital room where she found Will, camped on the floor, working on a laptop.

"Will?"

"Hey, Sara," he said, shoving his laptop into a briefcase and standing to greet her.

"What are you doing here?"

"I thought you might need a ride."

His wavy chestnut hair fell across his face, and he was wearing the same clothes he wore last night.

"You never left the hospital?" she said.

"Didn't have any place to be."

"What about your girls?"

"They're with their grandparents. I wasn't supposed to be home until the day after tomorrow anyway. I thought I'd let Nanny and Papa spoil them one more day."

"Where is—"

"Your protective detail? Officer Franklin's shift just ended and Nate left earlier this morning. He figured you'd be released today and apologized about not having the manpower to offer you protection 24/7. He was going to send an officer to drop you off wherever you needed to go, but I said I was already here. I could do it."

"Oh, he must have loved that," she said sarcastically.

"Yeah, well, I think he gave in because he knew it was a losing battle. So where can I drop you?"

"Really, that's not necessary. I can get a cab."

"What, do I smell that bad?" He sniffed his armpit teasingly.

"Stop," she said, almost smiling. "I appreciate the offer, but I think you've done enough."

"Miss Long?"

She turned and saw a police officer headed toward her.

"Yes?"

"I'm Officer Petrellis. I was sent to give you a ride."

"Officer, I'm Will Rankin." They shook hands. "Did Nate Walsh send you?"

"Yes, sir."

"Guess I lost that argument after all," Will said, frowning.

"Where can I drop you, ma'am?" Petrellis asked.

She looked reticent to tell him, so Will stepped in. "No, really, Officer, I insist."

"Detective Walsh said it's fine if you want to drive her,

but I need to follow to make sure she gets safely settled." He turned to Sara. "Ma'am, are you okay if Mr. Rankin gives you a ride?"

"Of course she is." Will turned to Sara. "Aren't you?"

She could tell from the expression on Will's kind face that it was important for him to do this, to help her. After everything she'd put him through, she didn't have it in her heart to disappoint him.

"Sure, that would be fine," she said.

Will motioned Sara toward the elevator.

She put on her emotional mask, needing to embody her undercover identity—Sara Long, tour guide assistant.

"We'll start by finding you a comfortable place to stay," Will said. "Nate suggested we book you a room at Echo Mountain Resort."

"Right, so he'll know where I am."

"No, because it's a very secure facility." They stepped into the elevator. Officer Petrellis joined them, but didn't participate in the conversation.

"They've had some experience protecting people at the resort," Will continued.

"Oh, really?" she said with a raised eyebrow.

"Long story. You hungry? We could stop for something to eat first."

"Actually, I desperately need a cell phone."

He pulled his smartphone out of his pocket and offered it to her. "It's working again."

"Thanks, but I need my own."

"Ah, calling your boyfriend, huh?"

She shrugged and decided not to answer, letting him draw his own conclusions. Having a boyfriend would certainly discourage Will from continuing to help her.

They stepped out of the elevator onto the main floor.

"What type of vehicle are you driving, sir?" Officer Petrellis asked Will. "In case we get separated."

"A gray Jeep."

"Plate number? Again, in case we get separated."

Will gave the plate number and the officer wrote it down. He was being awfully accommodating, Sara mused, especially since she was under the impression Nate didn't have the manpower to spare. But then this was small-town law enforcement. They were about building relationships and protecting their community.

"We can swing by the Super Shopper and get you a phone, some clothes and whatever else you need since you left your backpack up in the mountains," Will said.

She fingered the rip in her jacket. "That's probably a good idea. Tell me more about Echo Mountain Resort."

"It's on the outskirts of town," Will said. "I know a few people who work there, and the manager, as well. I'll give them a call to see what's available."

They went outside and headed for his Jeep.

"I feel bad that you're still involved in this, in my drama," she said.

"No worries. I want to see this through to the end."

Sara knew Will Rankin had no clue what he was signing on for.

Will called the resort. "Hi, Nia, it's Will. I have a friend who needs a room.…Wait, that's *this* weekend? I completely forgot…" He shot Sara a defeated look. "Okay, I'll try something in town.…I hope you're wrong about that.…Sure, I'll bring the girls by." He ended the call as they approached his truck.

"Bad news?" Sara asked.

"I forgot about the resort's big festival this weekend. It's booked solid. We'll try a B and B in town. How about we get you set up with a phone, and we'll make calls while we eat lunch? Sound good?"

"Sure."

He opened the door for her and she got into his Jeep. She noticed how he was careful to make sure she was settled before closing the door. He was the true definition of a gentleman, she thought, as she watched him walk around the front of the vehicle. What other kind of man would invest himself in a stranger's dangerous situation like Sara's?

One who, no doubt, had white knight syndrome tendencies. Well, she'd accept a ride from him, and buy him lunch to thank him for everything he'd done. Then, after he dropped her off at a B and B or wherever she ended up staying, she'd offer a firm goodbye.

They picked up supplies at the Super Shopper, and Sara made her call, but didn't look happy about the outcome. Will decided not to ask too many questions. He didn't want to push her away by being nosy.

Something still felt off, as if she acted a good game, but felt utterly alone, maybe even abandoned. Will decided he would not abandon Sara, then he cautioned himself not to feel so responsible for her.

He couldn't help it.

As they stood by his Jeep, she slipped on her new blue winter jacket and smiled at her reflection in the window. The smile lit her face, and he forced himself to look away. His gaze landed on the police officer's car a few parking spots away, reminding Will that Sara was still in danger.

"Well, I kinda like it," she said.

He snapped his attention to her. "I do, too."

"Then, why'd you look away?"

"Sorry, got distracted. Is it warm?"

"Yeah." She half chuckled.

"What's so funny?"

"You're such a dad."

"Is that a bad thing?" He opened the car door and she slid onto the front seat.

"No, but be warned, at some point with your girls it's going to be about looking good, not being warm."

"Don't remind me." He shut the door and went to the driver's side of the Jeep. He got behind the wheel and said, "You ready for lunch? There's this great new spot a few minutes away. My girls love it."

"What, is the menu all candy?" Sara teased.

Will pulled out of the lot. "Actually, it's called Healthy Eats." He smiled. "Don't let the name scare you."

"You're assuming I'm a junk-food person." She shifted in her seat and winced.

"Bad, huh?" he said.

"No, I'm fine. Looking forward to a nice room with a soft bed, and no police officers questioning me."

He understood her frustration, but she had killed a man in the mountains—to save Will's life. The primary reason he would not abandon her.

"There are three B and B's in town," Will started. "Annabelle's, Cedar Inn and The White Dove. Maybe you should give one of them a call?"

"Okay."

With each call, he could tell she grew more frustrated. A few minutes later they pulled into the lot at Healthy Eats.

"Don't worry," he said. "I know Lucy, the owner at The White Dove. They keep a spare room open in case her daughter shows up in town unexpectedly. I'll talk to her."

"Thanks."

Will sensed she was starting to fade. Food would definitely help renew her energy.

A few minutes later, they were seated in a booth ordering tea, scones and sandwiches from the owner of the restaurant, Catherine, who was Nate's sister.

"Shouldn't take long," Catherine said. "You two look as if you could use some of my healing broth. I'll bring some out, on the house."

"We really appreciate it, Catherine," Will said.

"Anything for you, Will." She winked and walked into the back.

"Someone's got a crush on you," Sara said.

"Who, Catherine? Nah, she's on the 'help Will' team."

"Help you what?"

"At first, it was to help me recover from my wife's death."

Sara reached across the table and touched the hand gripping his tea mug. "I'm so sorry, I did not mean to bring that up."

"It's okay. I've been grieving long enough. A lot of the folks in town, and especially from church, can't stop looking out for me. I'm blessed with good friends, yet sometimes..." His voice trailed off.

"Sometimes what?"

"All the attention can be suffocating. It makes me feel as if they think I'm incompetent." He didn't know why he said it, and wanted to take it back.

"You're the opposite of incompetent, Will," she offered. "Look at everything you've done for me."

"Thanks. I wasn't fishing for a compliment, honest."

She cracked a smile.

Again, he had to look away. That adorable smile of hers was enchanting. "I'll call Lucy about her daughter's room at The White Dove Inn."

"That would be great, thanks."

He pulled out his phone.

"Will? What are you doing here?"

Will looked up and spotted his in-laws crossing the restaurant toward him.

"And what happened to your eyes?" his mother-in-law, Mary, asked.

He got out of the booth to greet them. "Hiking accident," he said. Will shook hands with his father-in-law, Ed, who then went to the register to pick up their order.

"Where are the girls?" Will asked.

"Susanna Baker called and invited Claire and Marissa to join her and the twins for a movie." Mary studied Sara with judgment in her eyes.

"What movie?" Will asked. "Is it PG? Because the last PG-13 movie Marissa watched gave her nightmares."

"It's fine." Mary waved him off. "They were going to an animated film. Why are you back early? And who's this?"

He wouldn't sugarcoat it, nor would he go into great detail, either.

"Mary, this is Sara. I assisted Sara when she was injured in the mountains."

Sara offered Mary a smile. "Nice to meet you."

"Search and rescue…so that's what cut your vacation short," Mary said disapprovingly. "Are you expecting to pick up the girls tonight? Because we'd planned a trip to the children's museum tomorrow, and they were looking forward to tea at Queen Margaret tea shop."

"That's fine," Will said. "What time will you be dropping them home?"

"Between seven and seven-thirty."

"Sounds good. I'll be ready."

Mary cast one last look at Sara. "I most certainly hope so."

Ed joined them, gripping a to-go bag in his hand. "What'd I miss?"

"Will cut his trip short to save this young lady."

"Sara," she introduced herself.

"Ed, nice to meet you." He nodded at the bag. "I've worked up an appetite. Those girls never stop, do they?" He smiled at Will.

"No, they surely don't. Thanks again for watching them."

"Don't be silly," Mary said. "They're our granddaughters. We love them. You'll be home by seven tomorrow to greet the girls?"

"Of course," Will said.

"Goodbye, then." She turned and left.

Ed shrugged at Will and nodded at Sara. "Good to meet you."

"You, too."

Will watched them leave. Only after they'd pulled out of the lot did the tightening in his chest ease.

"Are you going to sit down?" Sara asked, with a question in her eyes.

"Yeah." He slid into the booth.

"What was that about?" Sara said.

"What?"

"She seemed awfully—"

"Judgmental? Critical? Close-minded?"

"Something like that." Sara smiled again.

The tension in his shoulders uncoiled. He shrugged. "It's complicated."

Catherine approached their table with soup. Good timing. He didn't want to get into the ugly story about how his in-laws had grown resentful of Will after Megan lost her battle with cancer, and how they questioned his abilities as a father.

"This is amazing," Sara said, spooning a second taste of soup.

They spent the next hour enjoying delicious food and natural conversation. He wasn't sure how that was possible, since he'd only known her for a day, yet he felt comfortable chatting about whatever topic drifted into their discussion.

He wondered if she also enjoyed their companionship. Then she offered to pay for his lunch and he wondered if this was her way of thanking him for saving her in the mountains, nothing more.

He called Lucy at The White Dove Inn and was able to secure Sara the room reserved for Lucy's daughter.

They finished their meal and he drove her across town to the inn, pointing out highlights of Echo Mountain, including the Christmas tree in the town square.

"We'll light it next weekend at the Town Lights Festival, not to be confused with the Echo Mountain Resort Festival," he said.

"Wow, there's a lot of celebrating going on for such a small town."

"There's a lot to celebrate this time of year," he offered.

She turned to look out the side window, as if she wasn't so

sure. In that moment, he pictured himself showing her how beautiful Christmas could be: drinking hot cider in the town square amongst friends and neighbors, attending Christmas church services and singing songs praising the Lord.

But Sara seemed lost in a dark memory, one he wished he could replace with new ones.

A few minutes later he pulled up in front of The White Dove Inn and Sara's eyes rounded with appreciation. "It's lovely."

He reached for his door.

"Don't."

He turned to her.

"Your journey ends here," she said.

"I'm confused. Did I somehow offend you?"

"No, nothing like that." She hesitated. "Let's face it, Will, it's in your best interest to steer clear of me."

"How do you figure?"

"I saw the way your mother-in-law looked at me, at this—" She motioned at the space between them. "I mean, I really appreciate everything you've done."

"But?"

"I need to ask you not to seek me out anymore."

"Seek you out? You make me sound like a stalker. I thought I was helping a friend."

"We don't know each other well enough to be friends. Maybe we could have been, if the situation were different."

"This has something to do with the call you made earlier, doesn't it?"

She didn't answer, glancing at him with sadness in her eyes. "You're a good man, Will. I wish you all the best." She leaned across the seat and kissed him on the cheek.

He couldn't breathe for a second, stunned by the kiss. She quickly grabbed her bag of supplies and hopped out of the Jeep, slamming the door and hurrying up the steps to the B and B.

She hesitated as she reached the door.

Turn around. Come on, change your mind, turn around and let me help you.

She didn't. She knocked on the door and a moment later it swung open. Lucy waved at Will over Sara's shoulder. He offered a halfhearted wave and Lucy shut the door.

Will glanced through his front windshield at the neighboring houses decorated in green, red and gold lights. Sara was right, of course, yet it still stung.

At first he thought he was drawn to her because she needed him, needed someone to take care of her, which was dysfunctional on so many levels. As he sat in his Jeep after being told to keep his distance, he realized it was something else that made him want to stay close.

He had connected with this stranger on a level he hadn't experienced with another woman since Megan. How was that possible?

"You're sleep deprived," he muttered, and pulled away from the curb.

He'd better catch up on his sleep if he wanted to be fresh and energized for the girls tomorrow. As he drove away from the B and B, he spotted the unmarked police car across the street. Officer Petrellis was on the phone, and nodded at Will as he passed.

Will was grateful that Nate had changed his mind about offering Sara protection, and decided to call him using his hands-free device.

"Will," Nate answered. "Was about to call you. Turns out the man Sara shot and killed had a rap sheet for assault and battery, and attempted murder, which he skated on thanks to high-priced attorneys he couldn't afford."

"You think LaRouche and Harrington paid the bill?"

"That'd be my guess. The DA doesn't see any reason to press charges against Sara for killing him in self-defense."

"That's great news. Listen, I wanted to thank you."

"For what?"

"For putting protective surveillance on Sara."

"Yeah, Spike's been sending me text updates all day."

"Spike? You mean Officer Petrellis."

"What are you talking about? Officer Petrellis took early retirement last spring."

SEVEN

A chill shot across Will's shoulders. "Petrellis said you sent him to protect Sara."

"No, Spike offered to give her a ride from the hospital to make up for messing up last night."

"I've gotta get back to Sara." Will spun the Jeep around. "I just dropped her off at The White Dove Inn."

"I'm on my way."

"How long will it take you to get there?"

"Five, maybe ten minutes."

"Hurry."

"Will, wait for me."

"I'll see you when you get there." Will ended the call, unable to agree to wait for Nate. It wasn't in Will's DNA to sit by and do nothing while someone stalked her.

He pulled up to the inn, a safe distance behind the unmarked cruiser. Drumming his fingers against the steering wheel, he peered into Officer Petrellis's car.

His empty car.

Will gripped the steering wheel with unusual force. Five minutes—he tried talking himself into waiting five minutes for Nate to arrive. He scanned the inn, studying every window for signs of trouble, then realized he wouldn't be able to see Sara from here since her room was by the dining room.

In the back where it was dark, where an intruder could easily sneak in unnoticed.

He was driving himself crazy sitting here, waiting for something to happen.

Worrying about what could happen.

Worrying about being too late.

He whipped open his door and took off toward the house. Would Petrellis harm Sara in front of an inn full of guests? No, he wouldn't be that bold. Besides, Will doubted the cop had been hired to hurt Sara. More likely he'd been ordered to get information and report back to the men who were after her.

Will decided to bypass the front entrance and enter through the back. As he walked along the dark side of the house, he saw a shadow up ahead, lit by a floodlight.

"Hey!" he called out.

The person turned around…

It was Lucy, owner of the inn.

"Hi, Will. What are you doing back here?"

"I wanted to check on Sara."

Lucy, in her late thirties, with short dark hair, planted her hands on her hips. "And you decided not to use the front door?"

"Sorry, I heard someone back here and thought I'd check it out."

"Just me, composting dinner scraps."

"Did a police officer stop by?"

"No, why? Am I in trouble?" she teased.

"Did you see anyone else out here tonight?"

"No, but then I wasn't looking." Her smile faded. "What's going on?"

"Let's go inside." He motioned her toward the house, hoping that Sara was okay.

As Will and Lucy climbed the back stairs, he scanned the property one last time before they went inside.

What if Petrellis had sneaked inside while Lucy was disposing of the dinner scraps?

"Maybe I should go in first," he offered.

Without argument, Lucy stepped aside and let him enter the kitchen. Pots and pans were stacked in the sink, and plates were lined up on the countertop.

No sign of Officer Petrellis.

"Sara's room is where?" he asked.

"Over here." Lucy led him through the dining room to a door off a small hallway.

He took a deep breath and tapped on her door. "Sara?"

No response.

"She said she was exhausted," Lucy offered.

He looked down at the soft glow reflecting from beneath the door.

Tapping harder, he called out, "Sara, it's Will. Are you all right?"

Again, silence.

"Please open the door," he said to Lucy.

"I don't feel right going into a guest's room while she's inside."

If she was still inside.

"It's an emergency," Will said. "I think she's in danger. While you were out back, someone could have made his way into her room."

The front doorbell rang repeatedly.

"That's probably Detective Walsh," Will said. "Go ahead and let him in. He'll explain the urgency."

With a worried nod, she went to greet Nate. Will continued to tap on the door. Maybe there was a simple explanation. Yeah, like she didn't want to talk to him. She'd said as much when she'd left his Jeep, right?

"Sara, please open the door," Will said.

Nate marched up to Will. "I told you to wait for me."

"Officer Petrellis wasn't in his car," Will said. "I couldn't wait, and now Sara's not answering her door."

Nate nodded at Lucy. "Please open it."

She pulled a master key out of her pocket. "Sara? We're sorry to intrude." She opened the door.

The room was empty.

Will noticed open French doors leading outside. "He took her."

Nate went to the doors, and turned to Lucy. "Where does this lead?"

"The driveway."

Nate checked the door. "Someone messed with the lock." Nate went outside to investigate.

Will couldn't move. The walls seemed to close in around him. His fault; this was his fault.

"Lucy, are you down here?" a guest called from the living room.

Lucy placed her hand on Will's shoulder. "I have to take care of my guest."

Maybe Will nodded, maybe he didn't. He couldn't be sure of anything right now, except for the fact he'd failed Sara.

As he struggled to calm his panicked thoughts, he noticed the backpack she'd bought at the Super Shopper beside the bed, plus the sneakers she'd worn out of the store. She'd been so happy to get out of the stiff, dirt-covered boots and into a pair of comfortable shoes.

She'd taken them off, and wore what out of here? The uncomfortable boots again? No, he didn't see that happening. Will snapped his attention to the armoire. He approached it and tapped gently with his knuckles.

"Sara, you in there?"

There was no response. He held his breath and cracked one of the doors open.

It was empty except for wood hangers and an ironing board.

"No one's outside." Nate came back into the room and shut the doors behind him. "And the sedan you described is gone. Spike's not answering my texts. I have to assume he wasn't sending the messages. Petrellis must have somehow gotten his phone. Hope Spike's okay." Nate patted Will's shoulder. "Hang in there, buddy. We'll find her."

"Okay." Will's mind raced with worst-case scenarios.

Nate hesitated before stepping out of the room. "This was not your fault, Will."

"Yeah, okay."

"I mean it." Nate left the room, his voice echoing across the first floor of the inn. "Base, this is Detective Walsh. I need you to ping Officer Spike Duggins's cruiser and get me that location. Also, send an officer to Stuart Petrellis's house, over."

As Will shut the doors to the armoire, he considered what could have happened. If Petrellis had broken into her room she wouldn't have gone willingly with him, and Will hadn't been gone that long, maybe five minutes, tops. He surely would have heard her protests.

Her cries for help.

His gaze drifted to her newly bought sneakers. Convinced she was still in the house, he went into the living area. Voices drifted from the kitchen, Lucy's voice, and another woman's—not Sara's.

Sara was hiding. He could feel it.

As he wandered through the living room, he noticed a door built into the wall beneath the stairs. His girls would definitely consider that the perfect hiding spot. Could Sara be in there? Or was he kidding himself, denying the reality of the situation?

The possibility that she'd been taken, and might be dead by morning.

Will went to the door and tapped gently.

"What are you doing?" Nate said, gripping his radio.

Will knocked again. "Sara, it's Will. You okay in there?"

A few tense moments of silence passed.

Please, Lord, give her the courage to open the door.

"I'm brewing tea," Lucy said from the kitchen doorway. "And warming scones."

"I needed a snack," her female guest said from the kitchen.

"Tea and scones, how about it, Sara?" Will tried again.

Either she was scared and hiding, or Will was making a complete fool of himself.

"Nate's here. You're safe," Will encouraged.

With a soft click, the closet door opened. Will offered his hand and Sara took it. As she stepped out, she glanced at Nate then at Lucy.

"Sorry," Sara said. She slipped her hand out of Will's and went to her room. Will and Nate followed.

"I'm so embarrassed," she said.

"What happened, and why were you in the closet?" Nate asked.

"I thought I saw a man outside my window. I was being paranoid."

"No, you're being careful," Will said. "And that's a good thing, right, Nate?"

"Yes. Especially given the circumstances."

"What circumstances?" Sara said, worry coloring her blue eyes.

"We'll explain on the way," Nate said.

"Where are we going?" she asked.

"We need to find you another safe house. Better yet, we've got an open cell at the station."

"No, you're not locking her up," Will said.

"For her own good," Nate argued.

"I've got a better idea."

It felt wrong on so many levels, Sara thought as she looked out the loft window to the parking area below. Will and Nate were outside having a heated discussion, probably about Sara, and why Will needed to stop helping her. Nate had been clear—Sara could remain free as long as she promised to stay in Echo Mountain until they finished investigating the stranger's death, and the supposed death of David Price.

Supposed, right.

To think that without Will's help Sara would be locked in a cell right now. Her gaze roamed the loft that his deceased wife had used as her art studio. It had a peaked ceiling with wood support beams, and lace curtains covering the rectangular windows. It was a peaceful place, a place where one could dream, imagine and create.

The loft wasn't meant to be used as a fortress.

It felt wrong to be here, not only because of the danger Sara brought with her, but also because of the lie she had to hide behind. Would Will see her differently if he knew the truth, that she was an FBI agent who'd failed miserably as she'd watched a man being murdered?

She didn't like lying to Will or the local authorities, but she wasn't ready to go public, not until she spoke with her supervisor. Unfortunately Bonner wasn't answering her calls. She wondered if it was a tough love thing, that he thought if he ignored her she'd get back to relaxing on a beach somewhere. Then she realized he wouldn't recognize the new phone number. She'd been hesitant to leave a message regarding the situation, she wasn't sure why. So she decided to keep trying until he picked up.

The last thing she wanted was to blow her cover and expose herself as FBI to LaRouche and Harrington. They'd surely destroy evidence that could be used to build a case against them.

Evidence. She felt in her pocket for her broken phone. She had to get it to a tech person and retrieve the recorded murder of David Price.

"How do I find one of those?" she whispered to herself.

Maybe she'd ask Will, since he seemed to know most everyone in town. Yes, she'd tell him she wanted to retrieve photos from her ruined phone.

She sighed, eyeing Will's commanding presence through the window as he spoke with Nate. She wanted to stop lying to Will, to the man who had continually offered support and encouragement. No man, besides her uncle, had ever done that for her. Most of the men she'd dated had seemed too self-absorbed, and the male agents at work were focused solely on their careers.

There was no room in the FBI for weakness. She thought she'd covered hers pretty well with sheer grit and determination to nail criminals. Instead, Bonner criticized her for her tenacity, saying it had gotten her into trouble, that she saw crimes where there were none. He even insinuated she was overcompensating for something, like her small stature or even…

A past failure.

That seemed like a low blow, considering Bonner knew about her father's death.

She stepped away from the window and unzipped her backpack, still frustrated with herself for hiding when she felt the threat looming outside her room at the inn. She should have stood up for herself and taken the guy down. Any other FBI agent would have detained him for questioning.

"Yeah, with bruised ribs and a sprained wrist?"

The sound of footsteps echoed against the stairs. Putting distance between her and Will was getting more and more difficult, especially since she was staying in his wife's art studio.

That's not the only reason, Sara.

She felt herself opening up to him, allowing herself to be vulnerable for the first time since…

Had she ever really been vulnerable to a man before?

"It's not a five-star hotel, but it's pretty nice, huh?" Will said, stepping up to the top floor.

"It's charming." She glanced at him. "But I don't like putting you or your family in danger."

"You aren't. This place is a few blocks from my house, and isn't in my name, so no one will be able to make the connection between us."

"Who owns it?"

"A couple that travels ten months out of the year. I'd agreed to maintain things around here in exchange for Megan's use of the loft. I kept doing it, you know, as a favor."

Sara suspected it was more than that. She suspected he liked being around his wife's former space.

"The daybed isn't bad," he said. "Megan spent her share of nights here." He looked away, as if he hadn't meant to admit that.

"I'm sorry," she said.

He frowned. "Why?"

"You two were having trouble?"

"No, it wasn't that…well, not initially. It was the cancer. She wanted to spend the last few months here with the caregiver so I could get used to raising the girls alone. At least that's what she said."

"That must have been rough."

"Yeah, well, we had the loft cleaned out, so no cancer germs," he joked. He closed his eyes and sighed. "I don't know where that came from. I'm sorry."

"You don't need to apologize. You've been through a lot, and you have a right to react any way you want."

"Yeah, but that made me sound like a heartless jerk."

"Not even on your worst day could anyone think of you as a heartless jerk."

Will snapped his gaze to hers. Sara felt her heartbeat tapping against her chest.

Don't do this, Sara. He's a man still grieving for his wife, and you happen to be standing in her space.

"Hopefully a room will open up at the resort in the next day or two and I can move over there." She refocused on emptying her backpack of clothes and setting them on a wooden bench. "Oh, I meant to ask if you knew of a place in town where I could get my phone looked at?"

"The new one?"

"No, my original phone. It was damaged in the fall and I'd like to retrieve things from it, like pictures."

"I know a techie who could help."

"Great, thanks."

"Nate has assigned a police officer to keep watch."

"What about Spike, the one who Nate thought was looking after me?"

"They found him wandering by the highway, disoriented, and took him to the hospital."

"Officer Petrellis did that to him?"

"Nate suspects so, yes, and that Petrellis took Spike's phone and was texting updates to Nate."

"Is Spike okay?"

"He'll be fine. He's a tough kid who came on the force a few months ago. He's probably wondering if that was such a good idea right about now."

"Did they track down Petrellis?"

"No one was home when they checked his house. No car in the driveway, and the blinds were all closed. They've got a bulletin out on him. Anyway, a police officer should be arriving shortly to keep an eye on things here."

"I thought Nate didn't have the resources, or are they worried I'll flee the county?"

"Nate is concerned about your safety."

She nodded, hoping the detective truly believed her.

"Sara?"

"I'm fine. You don't have to stay."

"Okay, well…" He ran an anxious hand through thick chestnut hair. "There are fresh towels in the bathroom, and you bought toiletries at the store so you should be all set."

"Yep, looking forward to a good night's sleep."

"Okay, well, until tomorrow."

"Will, you don't have to—"

"Don't tell me not to check on you, Sara."

"You're awfully determined."

"Sometimes not determined enough. I won't make that mistake again."

She frowned, trying to figure out what he meant.

"Have a good night," he said in a firm voice. "The door automatically locks when I shut it. You can flip the deadbolt if you want, as well."

"Okay, thanks."

With a nod, he went downstairs and shut the door with a click.

She felt so alone in this strange place, a place where Will's wife had withdrawn from the world, which was kind of what Sara felt as though she was doing.

She could neither withdraw from the world, nor her current situation. There was a case to solve, two men to put away for murder, at the very least.

She pulled out her newly purchased cell phone and called her boss, this time deciding to leave a message.

"This is Agent Bonner. Leave a message."

"It's Agent Vaughn. There's been a development in the LHP case and I need to speak with you immediately. Here is my new number." She rattled it off. "The suspected drug case is now first-degree murder. I witnessed LaRouche kill David Price."

She ended the call and stared at the phone. That should get him to call her back.

Exhaustion took hold, and she flopped down on the daybed. The echo of car doors slammed outside, and she figured the new surveillance officer had arrived.

Sara took a deep breath and relaxed, knowing she'd think more clearly after a decent night's sleep. She felt safe for now. No one knew where she was. LaRouche and Harrington couldn't find her here.

She sighed and drifted off to sleep.

Sara awoke with a start. She wasn't sure how long she'd been asleep, perhaps not long because it was still dark outside. She grabbed her phone. It was nearly ten.

Then she heard what had awakened her: the creak of wooden floorboards. Someone was coming up the steps.

Sara sat up, her heart racing. She'd left the desk lamp on, which she often did, so she wouldn't be disoriented if she awakened. She searched the room for a closet, a place to hide.

No, she wouldn't keep hiding like a coward, a weak and fragile woman who didn't belong in the field. But she needed a better position from which to defend herself.

She noticed a rock candleholder on the desk across the room. She grabbed it and crouched beside a set of file cabinets.

Her attacker was pretty smart to have eluded the police officer outside. Was Petrellis coming up the stairs? She bit her lower lip with worry, remembering he was at least six feet tall. Sure, she could call 911, only they wouldn't get here in time to prevent the assault. They'd arrive after the fact, after she'd been taken, or beaten up, or worse.

She focused on the sound. Silence rang in her ears. Was she was imagining things?

No, she wouldn't be swayed by her boss's comment that, at times, her overzealousness bordered on irrational.

Another creak of floorboards echoed across the loft.

Focus, Sara. Breathe.

Creak, creak.

Now it sounded as though the creak was coming from the other side of the loft.

The intruder was up here, with Sara. Coming closer.

Closer.

Weapon in hand, Sara waited…

EIGHT

Will had drifted off to sleep on the sofa when the phone awakened him.

"Yeah?" he said.

"Is Claire with you?" his mother-in-law said.

"What?" He sat up.

"Susanna can't find her. She thinks she might have gone home."

The phone pressed to his ear, Will searched the house. The beds were neatly made. No Claire. "She's not here. What happened?"

"Claire got upset and Susanna thought she went into the bedroom, but now she can't find her. One of the girls thought she heard her go out the back."

"I'll go look for her. She shouldn't be walking around at night."

"You're preaching to the choir. That girl should be grounded for life."

"I'll call when I find her." He pocketed his phone, grabbed his house keys and headed outside, figuring he'd walk to Susanna's house and hopefully run into his daughter making her way home.

He tamped down the panic, knowing it was a senseless emotion, yet a natural one. What happened that upset Claire? She'd been moody lately, and he wondered if something was happening with her friends or at school, and she couldn't bring herself to talk to Will about it. Listening and giving advice had always been Megan's role.

He walked a few blocks and automatically glanced to his

right, across the park at the house with the upstairs loft that his wife, and now Sara, used as a refuge.

A shriek echoed across the park.

More lights popped on in the loft.

And a little person sprinted out of the house, past the patrol car parked out front.

Claire?

He took off toward her. What was she doing at the loft? Unless…

She missed her mom.

And found a stranger in her mother's space.

That must have been confusing, not to mention frightening for his daughter.

Will caught up to her on the lake path.

"Daddy! Daddy!" she sobbed.

Will whisked her into his arms. "Hey, baby girl. It's okay. I'm here."

"There was a…ghost in the loft!"

"No, honey, there's no such thing as a ghost."

"I saw her!"

She continued to sob against his shoulder and he debated taking her home, or going back to the loft to clear this up. A uniformed police officer headed toward them. The one thing Will did not want was for Sara's protective detail to leave his post.

Carrying Claire in his arms, Will headed toward the loft.

"Where are we going?" Claire said.

"To show you it wasn't a ghost, then I'll take you home. What were you doing at the loft anyway?"

"Nothing."

"Claire Renee Rankin."

A few seconds passed, then she said, "I go there sometimes, that's all."

"You go inside?"

"Yeah. I found a secret way inside."

He approached the police officer and recognized Officer Ryan McBride, Bree's cousin. "Hi, Ryan," Will said.

"I didn't even see her until she came racing out of the house. Is she okay?"

"Yeah, just scared. What about Sara?"

They both turned to look at the house. Sara stood in the doorway on the first floor, gripping a blanket around her shoulders.

"See, that's the ghost!" Claire cried into Will's shoulder.

"No, honey. That's Sara, a friend of mine," Will said. "I'm sure she feels badly about scaring you. Let's go talk to her."

Claire shook her head no.

"Look, you weren't supposed to be at the loft in the first place, were you?"

She shook her head again.

"Okay, then, let's face the consequences of your actions and sort this out." He nodded at Officer McBride and continued to the house.

"Will, I'm so sorry. I thought it was an intruder," Sara said, pulling the blanket tight around her shoulders with one hand.

"Let's go inside."

The three of them went upstairs. Will sat on a gray wingback chair and adjusted Claire on his lap. His little girl buried her face against his shoulder.

Sara sat on the daybed across the room. "I'm so sorry," she repeated.

"So is Claire, aren't you, baby girl?" Will said.

"I'm not a baby anymore, Daddy."

"No? So you're a big girl, and big girls can run off without telling anyone where they're going?"

She didn't answer.

"What happened, sweetheart?" he said, softening his voice.

"Nothing."

"Claire?" he pushed.

"We were making cookies."

"And…?"

"Olivia wanted to make snicker doodles, and Marissa said, you mean snicker poodles."

"That upset you because…?"

She leaned back and looked at him. "Those are Mommy's special cookies."

"Right. And it made you miss your mom?"

She buried her face against his neck. "It made me sad, so I went for a walk. Don't be mad, Daddy."

"I'm not angry. I was worried. So was your grandmother, Mrs. Baker, and what about your little sister? Remember the buddy system? You're never supposed to leave her alone."

"She was eating cookie dough. She didn't care."

"Of course she did. As a matter of fact, I'd better call over there. First, let me introduce you to my friend, Miss Sara. She was hurt in a hiking accident and SAR rescued her. I offered to let her stay here."

"This is Mommy's place," Claire's muffled voice said.

"I know, but Mommy's not using it right now, and Miss Sara needs a place to sleep." He shot a half smile across the room at Sara.

Sara's gaze was intent on the back of Claire's head.

"How about it?" Will said. "Can we show Miss Sara our gracious hospitality by letting her stay here for a few days?"

"I guess." Claire leaned back and looked at Will. "What happened to your face, Daddy?"

"I had a hiking accident, too."

"Did they have to rescue you?"

"No, I walked down on my own."

"You look like you were in a fight."

"Do I look like I won?" he teased.

"Yeah." Claire giggled.

"Good answer," he said. "Now, I'd better call your grandmother before she sends out the National Guard." Will shifted Claire off his lap and made the call.

* * *

By holding the blanket loosely around her body, Sara managed to hide the fact that she was still trembling. The adrenaline rush hadn't worn off from the past few minutes.

Will's daughter studied her with fascination and fear coloring her eyes. To think Sara had nearly conked the girl on the head with the rock candle.

Yet she hadn't because as Sara had been about to jump out of her hiding spot, the little girl had whispered, "Mommy, where are you?"

Sara had put down her weapon and stepped out from behind the file cabinet. Unfortunately revealing herself had terrified little Claire.

Mommy, where are you?

Hadn't Sara asked the same question a hundred times as a child? Wondering why her mom had had to go live at the hospital, and then why she'd never come home.

Sara's heart ached for Claire.

"It's fine. She's fine," Will said into the phone.

Sara noticed how he inadvertently stroked Claire's hair while speaking to his mother-in-law.

Claire hadn't taken her eyes off Sara.

"I'm sorry if I frightened you," Sara said.

"Why were you hiding?"

"I was scared."

"Of me?" Claire said, incredulously.

"I didn't know it was you," Sara explained. "All I heard was someone coming up the steps."

"Oh," Claire said, thinking for a minute on that one. "Can you draw?"

Sara bit back a smile at the random nature of her question. "No, not really."

"Mommy says everyone can draw."

"She created wonderful things." Sara eyed the sketches pinned to the walls.

"No, I'll take her home and pick up Marissa on the way,"

Will said into the phone. "I think she should be grounded, don't you?" He glanced at Claire.

His daughter shook her head no, that she didn't want to be grounded.

"Nonrefundable, huh?" Will continued. "Okay, I guess you can swing by in the morning and pick them up… See you then." Will pocketed his phone and looked at Claire. "Nanny and Papa spent a lot of money on tickets to the museum, so I'm going to let you go with them tomorrow, and then tomorrow night we'll talk about the consequences of your actions."

"Don't ground me next week, please, Daddy. It's after-school art camp."

"We'll talk about it later."

The little girl looked as if she was going to burst into another round of tears. Sara did not envy Will's job of being a single parent.

"Let's go," he said, reaching out for Claire. "Sara needs to get some sleep."

Claire ignored her father's hand and studied her shoes.

"Claire?" Will prompted.

"Whenever I come here—" she hesitated "—I usually say a prayer for Mommy."

Will's expression softened. "Good idea."

Claire pressed her fingers together in prayer, as did Will.

Sara hadn't prayed since…well, she couldn't remember the last time she'd prayed. She figured, why bother? It hadn't helped when Mom was sick, and what kind of God would take Sara's father away from her?

"Don't you know how to pray?" Claire asked Sara with a frown. "It's easy. You put your hands together, see?" She nodded at her own fingers.

Sara had to stop thinking about her own pain and consider little Claire's emotional recovery. Sara pressed her hands together, the feeling so awkward and uncomfortable. "Like this?"

"Yes, then close your eyes."

Sara did as requested. How could anyone deny such a sweet little girl who was still grieving for her mom?

"Dear Lord," Claire began. "Take good care of my Mommy because she always took good care of us. I hope she's helping you in Heaven, and I hope she'll never forget us. I love you, Mommy. Amen."

"Amen," Sara and Will said in unison.

She didn't know about Will, but Sara could hardly speak past the ball of emotion in her throat.

"Good," Will said in a rough voice. "Good prayer."

"You did good, too, Miss Sara," Claire offered.

"Thank you."

Claire went to take her father's hand.

"Hopefully there won't be any more excitement," Will said to Sara. "I'll see you tomorrow."

"You don't—"

"I'll bring breakfast by after my in-laws pick up the girls."

"We want to come for breakfast," Claire said. "Please, Daddy, please?"

"Enough, sweetheart. Let's get your sister and go home. We'll figure out the rest tomorrow."

Claire grinned. Sara wondered if the little girl had Will wrapped around her finger.

"Until tomorrow, then." Will escorted Claire to the top of the stairs.

"Good night, Will," Sara said. "Sweet dreams, Claire."

Claire smiled at Sara. "I'll say a prayer for you tonight so you won't be scared anymore."

Claire started down the stairs and Will glanced at Sara.

"She's adorable," Sara said.

"Yeah."

With an odd, almost sad smile, Will disappeared down the stairs with his daughter.

After everything that had happened today and this evening, Sara realized spending time with Will and his girls for breakfast tomorrow was a horrible idea. She'd be hiding behind a shield of lies, and that was starting to feel terribly wrong.

As she stretched out on the bed, she heard Claire's prayer: *Take good care of my Mommy because she always took good care of us.*

That was what Will and his girls needed most: someone to take care of them. Sara was a dangerous diversion from that goal, although Will didn't know how dangerous.

She felt something brewing between she and Will: a closeness, a connection. She couldn't let that happen.

"Stop thinking about them."

No matter how much a part of her enjoyed watching Will interact with Claire, listening to Claire pray for her mother and taking refuge in the loft, the reality was, Sara had a job to do. If only her boss would call her back.

Until then, she had to stop involving innocents like Will and his girls, for their own good.

Sara got up early the next morning and tried to leave, but Officer McBride asked her to wait until Nate arrived. Asked? More like ordered her to stay put, up in her tower.

Sara could have argued, but she wasn't an idiot. Making enemies with the local cops wasn't a great idea, especially since she'd need their support, not their suspicions.

As she gazed out the window, she imagined what it would be like to live in a small town like Echo Mountain. Sara had hopped from one place to another after high school, first switching colleges to get the best criminal justice degree, then taking jobs to support her goal of becoming an FBI agent.

Yet life seemed so peaceful in Echo Mountain.

She sighed. Things always looked different from the outside. Like the bureau, and how it was nothing like she'd imagined. They didn't rush out and nail the bad guys. They had to follow protocol and procedure, and sometimes that meant a criminal wouldn't be prosecuted.

As she gazed at the mountain range in the distance, she wondered if LaRouche and Harrington had come down from the mountain, and what story they'd tell.

She spotted Will's Jeep cross the property. He parked and got out, with both little girls in tow.

"Will, no," she said. Bringing the girls here would only make things harder.

He carried what looked like a pastry box. Sara couldn't believe he'd awakened his daughters this early to bring her breakfast.

"Sara?" Will called from the bottom of the stairs.

"Come on up!" It's not as if she could turn them away. She wouldn't be that cruel, especially not to two little ones.

Will, Claire and her little sister came up to the loft. "Marissa, this is Miss Sara," Will introduced.

"You look like Mommy," Marissa said matter-of-factly.

"She does not," Claire argued.

"Girls," Will said. "Show Miss Sara what we brought her."

Claire shook her head disapprovingly at her little sister, then placed a box on the desk. She opened it slowly, reverently, as if she was showing off the crown jewels instead of creatively designed pastries. "These are Maple Bars, these are Chocolate Chipmunk Bars and these are Penelope's Pink Pansies."

Marissa leaned over the box, her green eyes widening. She looked a lot like her father. "Pansies are my favorite."

"I'm guessing these didn't come from Healthy Eats," Sara said.

"You'd guess right." Will smiled.

"We only get these on special occasions," Claire explained.

"Yeah, special occasions," Marissa echoed.

Was that what this was, a special occasion? Sara was in deeper trouble than she thought.

"Wow, how do I rate?" she asked Will.

"Thought it might help your aches and pains. Here." He pulled napkins out of his pocket and put them on the desk. "We're calling this first breakfast."

"Yeah, because Papa likes to eat breakfast out so we'll have second breakfast with him," Marissa said, licking the frosting off her Pink Pansy pastry.

For a brief second, Sara enjoyed the warmth of family, of children. In that moment, she shoved aside all thoughts of LaRouche and Harrington.

She reminded herself that this, the smiles of little girls licking frosting off their lips, was only an illusion, one that would evaporate soon enough.

Claire lifted a doughnut out of the box and raised it to her lips, eyes rounding with delight.

"It's terrifying, isn't it?" Will said.

Sara looked at him. "What?"

"The expression on her face when she's about to eat copious amounts of sugar and fat."

"If you think that's terrifying, how about this?" Sara grabbed a Maple Bar, took a bite and rolled her eyes from side to side, and up and down.

The girls giggled.

"You look crazy," little Marissa said.

"She looks happy," Claire countered.

"Happy doesn't look like this." Marissa imitated Sara. "It looks like this." Marissa cracked a broad grin, exposing frosting on her teeth.

"Gross. You are so immature," Claire said.

"I'm not manure."

"I didn't say..." Claire sighed. "Oh, never mind."

Will and Sara shared a smile.

"Tell Miss Sara where you're going today," Will said, plucking a chocolate doughnut for himself.

"A doll museum," Claire said with awe in her voice. "They have dolls from all over the world. Even Russia."

"Is that far away?" Marissa said.

"Of course it is," Claire countered.

"How do you know? Have you been there?"

"You know I haven't been there."

"Then, how do you know it's far away?"

"I learned it in school, silly."

"Oh." Marissa thought for a second, then looked at Sara. "Do you draw?"

"No, not really."

Marissa looked at her sister. "Mommy said—"

"Miss Sara hasn't learned yet," Claire explained.

"Let's teach her." Marissa scrambled off her chair and rushed to the other side of the room. She grabbed a sketch pad and dashed back to her sister.

"Pencils?" Claire said.

Again, Marissa raced across the room, went to a shelf and snatched a few pencils.

"Good." Claire cracked her knuckles.

This was quite the operation, Sara mused.

Claire nodded at the doughnut in Sara's hand. "You'll have to put down the doughnut."

"Right." Sara laid it on a napkin and brushed off her hands.

"Hold the pencil between your fingers like this." Claire demonstrated. "Watch me."

Marissa studied her sister and mimicked her every move.

Sara caught Will's expression, a mixture of pride and sadness, punctuated with a thoughtful smile. Drawing obviously reminded him of his wife.

"Then you draw a *t* in the middle of the page."

"Why are you drawing a *t*?" Sara said.

"It's how you draw a face. You connect the corners." Claire nibbled her lower lip. Marissa imitated the motion of drawing a circle. "And there you have the outline of the lady's head." Claire held up the sketchpad.

"Why are you drawing a lady?" Marissa asked.

"Men are boring. Ladies have hair and makeup and fun stuff like that," she answered her sister. She pointed to her drawing. "Then you'll draw the eyes here." Claire pointed. "See, the eyes are above the cross line, like on a real face. You try." Claire handed Sara a pencil.

Sara made a *t* and drew an oval shape by connecting the tips of the letter.

"That's good, now make the eyes," Claire said.

Will's phone buzzed.

"Whoops, that's Nanny and Papa. They're wondering where you are. Let's go, girls."

The girls grabbed their doughnuts and headed for the stairs. Claire turned to Sara. "Don't eat all the Pink Pansies or you'll get a tummy ache."

"Okay, I won't." Sara smiled.

"I'll be back in twenty," Will said.

"I'll be here, practicing my drawing."

Marissa ran up and hugged Sara's legs. "Don't worry. You'll be able to draw someday."

So stunned by the display of affection, Sara didn't immediately return the hug. Her heart sank. She never realized what she'd been missing. Just as she wrapped her arms around the little girl, Marissa sprung free and skipped up to her dad and sister.

"Dolls, dolls, dolls!" Marissa chanted.

Will cast one last smile at Sara and led the girls downstairs. Sara went to the window. She watched them get into Will's Jeep and pull away.

An ache permeated her chest. They were such a lovely family: a protective, gentle father and two sweet, albeit precocious little girls. Will's family seemed so perfect, so…

She turned back to the room. How could they be so grounded and at peace after having lost a mother, a wife?

Sara wandered to the table where they had practiced drawing. A day hadn't gone by since her father's murder that Sara hadn't felt the burn of anger.

The Rankin family had suffered a great loss, but didn't seem to let the grief shadow their conversations.

Their every thought.

All of Sara's decisions since Dad's death had been motivated by anger and the need for justice. Get a criminal justice degree, work her way into a job with the FBI and hunt down bad guys and put them behind bars.

Make them pay.

Because her dad's killer was never caught, never served his time.

Now, in her thirties, Sara was all about her career. She had no personal life, no boyfriend or even close friends for that matter. She never had time to nurture those kinds of relationships.

Being with Will and his girls, seeing how the community rallied around him and protected him, triggered an ache in Sara's chest for that which she would never have.

"One more reason you need to get out of here." She grabbed her backpack and considered her options. If Officer McBride wouldn't allow her to leave until she spoke with Nate, perhaps she could talk him into taking her to the police station to wait this out. One thing was for sure—staying here, in Will's deceased wife's studio, was messing with Sara's head. Big-time.

She glanced around the loft to make sure she hadn't forgotten anything. Her gaze landed on a photo of Will's wife with an arm around each of her little girls. Sara had a photo a lot like that one, of Sara, her dad and little brother, Kenny. It was taken at the beach. They were happy, laughing.

A perfect moment lost in the chaos of murder.

You and your brother hide in the closet. Do not come out until I say it's okay.

The slamming of a car door outside ripped her out of the

memory. Time to distance herself from Will and his girls. It was stirring up too many memories and buried grief.

Grief she'd been able to neutralize with determination to get justice.

She headed downstairs, deciding she'd sleep in a cell if she had to. She'd be safe at the police station, and a lot safer emotionally than if she continued to stay here.

As she headed for the patrol car, she saw Detective Walsh talking on his phone. He didn't look happy. Then he shot her a look, and she slowed her step. Something was very wrong.

"I understand. Text me the coordinates and I'll pass them along to SAR. We'll send a team. Once they're down I'll want to interview each of them individually.…Yes, I have her in custody."

In custody? Sara dug her fingers into the strap of her backpack.

Nate ended the call and turned to Sara. "Mr. LaRouche and Mr. Harrington finally called in. They said David Price disappeared after he got into an argument with you."

NINE

"What?" Sara said in disbelief.

"They claim the last time they saw Mr. Price, you two were arguing over money."

"Unbelievable," she muttered.

"Is it true? You were arguing about money and, what, he fell?"

"Absolutely not."

"Just the same, I need you to come with me to the station."

Her heartbeat sped up. "Are you arresting me?"

"I'm bringing you in for questioning."

"They're lying. I don't care about money," she ground out. "I only care about..."

Don't say it. Not yet.

"Ma'am?" Detective Walsh prompted.

"Forget it." Of course they'd pin the murder on her. It was an easy solution to fix their problems. And they'd get away with it. They'd discredit Sara and make her a viable suspect.

"Is there anything you want to tell me?" Nate asked.

She clenched her jaw, wanting to tell the detective who she really was. Sara feared losing traction with this case if word got out and LaRouche and Harrington discovered she was FBI.

She noticed Will's Jeep heading toward them. Perfect. This would drive him away, Will and his adorable girls, girls who didn't need to be exposed to the ugliness of Sara's life.

"Do what you have to do," she said to Nate.

Nate studied her with creased eyebrows. "Let's go." He motioned for her to get into his unmarked squad car.

Will pulled up beside them and hopped out. "Hey, what's going on?"

"I've been accused of murder," Sara said. "Okay? I'm dangerous. Stay away from me."

She climbed into the car and Nate shut the door. She couldn't hear what they were saying because they'd stepped away from the car, but she could tell Will argued fiercely with the detective.

Finally, Nate shook his head in frustration and got into the car.

She stared at the headrest of the seat in front of her, trying to block out Will's presence. He tapped on her window and she glanced out at his confused face. He looked as if he wanted answers.

As if he deserved answers.

She ripped her gaze from his emerald eyes. "Are we going or what?"

As Nate pulled away, Sara's eyes watered. *Goodbye, Will.*

She felt utterly alone. She wasn't working in an official capacity for the FBI, her supervisor hadn't returned her calls and now she'd pushed away the one person who truly wanted to help her.

"He deserves the truth."

She snapped her eyes to the back of Nate's head. "Meaning what?"

"Will saved your life and put himself at risk by protecting you. Don't you think that deserves complete honesty?"

"It doesn't matter."

"Oh, yes, ma'am, it does. Will Rankin is one of the most honorable men I know. For some strange reason he's decided you're worthy of his protection. He's usually got good instincts about people."

She gazed out the window as they passed a park filled with children.

"So? Were his instincts right about you?" Nate pushed.

She sighed. If LaRouche and Harrington were going to

frame her, she'd better get ahead of this thing and confide in the local police.

"Yes, his instincts are good."

"And?"

"I'm FBI."

"Really," he said, disbelief in his voice.

"Yes."

"And you didn't bother to tell me or Will that before now because…?"

"I'm undercover."

"Then, you should have brought me into your investigation." Nate got a call and answered his radio. "Detective Walsh, go ahead, over."

"Someone saw Petrellis at the Super Shopper, about half an hour ago, over."

"He's still in town?" Nate muttered to himself, then responded into the radio, "Send a unit to check it out. If the officer sees Petrellis, he needs to call for backup. Do not approach him alone, over."

"Ten-four."

He clicked off the radio and eyed her in the rearview. "We'll finish our discussion at the station."

Nate focused on driving, visibly frustrated by the call.

"You think he should have left town?" she said.

"Wouldn't you? I mean, we suspect that he drugged Spike, and was following you around all day for some nefarious reason."

"What happened with Spike, exactly?"

"Petrellis saw him outside the hospital and approached him, acting as though they're buddies. He congratulated Spike on the new job with Echo Mountain PD and slapped him on the shoulder. Hard. Spike says he thought he felt a pinch, like a bee sting. That's pretty much all he remembers." Nate shook his head. "What is happening to my town?"

Sara gazed out the window, feeling even guiltier that she brought trouble to the community of Echo Mountain.

* * *

Within minutes Will was on the phone calling Royce Burnside, the best lawyer in Echo County. Will had done search engine optimization marketing work for Royce's law firm and knew of their stellar reputation.

As a favor to Will, Royce said he'd meet him at the police station right after lunch. Will stopped himself from marching into the station alone, all fired up. He worked on marketing projects for the next few hours in his home office. Unfortunately, the image of a bruised and fragile Sara being aggressively interrogated kept seeping into his thoughts, distracting him.

Will leaned back in his chair and pulled his fingers off the keyboard. What was Nate thinking? Sara wasn't a criminal or a violent woman. She'd gone into shock after shooting a man, and had experienced traumatic flashbacks.

Although he sensed that Sara wanted to go this alone, the more she pushed Will away, the more determined he was to help. Sure, he knew once this case was resolved and she was given her freedom, she'd probably leave town and he'd never see her again. It didn't matter. She needed help and he wanted to be the one to give it to her.

He warmed up butternut-squash soup from Healthy Eats for lunch, hoping Nate at least had the decency to feed Sara. Maybe Will would bring some soup just in case. He had plenty.

Minutes stretched like hours as he waited for one o'clock.

"This is ridiculous." Although it was only twelve fifteen, he packed up a container of soup, grabbed a small bag of crackers and headed for the station. He brought his laptop as well, figuring he'd get some work done while waiting for Royce.

Will wasn't even sure Sara needed an attorney, but it wouldn't hurt to have one in her corner.

He parked in the lot, pulled out his laptop and moved his seat back so he could open it up and work. The whole work thing lasted about five minutes. Glancing at the building and knowing she was inside being questioned about a murder she didn't commit drove Will nuts.

Some folks would call him nuts for believing in a complete stranger.

But they weren't strangers. She'd exposed herself to him in a way he suspected she hadn't with many, if anyone. When she'd hidden under the bed, clutching the blanket to her chest, she'd seemed like a child, fearing for her life.

Something terrible had happened to Sara in her past, and it had all come rushing back after the shooting.

Will tucked the laptop into his backpack and grabbed the soup bag. He didn't care if he was early. He'd text Royce to meet him inside.

As he headed for thc building, he spotted a familiar car parked across the street from the police station.

Officer Petrellis's unmarked sedan.

Surprised and concerned, Will glanced away, so as not to be obvious. He pulled out his phone and texted Nate about the car. They were looking for the retired officer to question him about yesterday, about drugging Spike and stalking Sara.

"Hello, Mr. Rankin."

Will glanced up. Petrellis was heading toward him.

"Officer," Will greeted, then hit Send on the text to Nate.

"What brings you to the station?" Petrellis said.

"Visiting my friend Nate."

"And what about your other friend Sara? How is she doing?"

"I wouldn't know. I've been busy with work."

"How well do you know her, if you don't mind my asking?"

"I don't know her at all, actually. I helped rescue her after a nasty fall. That's it." He glanced at his watch. "Whoa, I'm late. Excuse me."

Will turned to walk away, to put distance between him and the retired officer with questionable motivations.

Something stabbed Will in the arm and he instinctively jerked back. "Hey!"

"You need to come with me."

"Excuse me?"

"I need to ask you some questions."

"I don't have time. I've got to get inside and…and…" Ringing started in his ears, and his surroundings went in and out of focus.

"Here, let me help you." A firm hand gripped Will's arm and led him away from the police station, away from Sara.

"No." Will yanked his arm away. "I have to talk to her."

"Her? You mean Sara?"

A part of Will knew he'd said too much. His brain was floating on some kind of wave, pulling him away from the shoreline of reality.

They found Spike wandering the highway, Nate had told Will.

That must be what was happening to Will.

"Relax," Petrellis said as they approached his car. "It will be over soon."

Over? As in…

Was Petrellis going to kill him? Leaving the girls with no parents, and judgmental grandparents to raise them?

"No!" Will shouldered Petrellis against the car and fired off punches.

"Will!" Nate called from across the street.

Petrellis yanked Will forward, kneed him in the gut and cast him aside. Will collapsed on the pavement and watched Petrellis's car speed off.

"No," Will croaked, wanting Petrellis to come back, to tell them why he was after Sara.

Sara. The beautiful woman with the big blue eyes.

"Will." It was Sara's voice.

He looked up, into her worried eyes.

"No, I want all patrols to be on the lookout," Nate's voice said from behind her. "He's headed south on Main Street toward the interstate, over."

"Will?" Nate said.

All Will could see were Sara's blue eyes.

"Nate didn't arrest you, did he?" Will asked her.

"No." She placed a comforting hand on his chest. "What happened?"

"Dispatch, I need an ambulance," Nate's voice said.

"No," Will said. "No ambulance."

"Will, you're hurt," Nate argued.

"Drugged like Spike. Felt him stick my arm."

"Then, an ambulance can take you to the hospital."

"Everyone will know. My in-laws—"

"This wasn't your fault," Sara said.

"Stop worrying about them, Will," Nate said. "The ambulance will be here shortly."

"Have to get home… The girls."

"They're not coming home until seven, remember?" Sara offered. "It's only twelve-thirty."

"Oh, yeah." He closed his eyes, then opened them again. "Are you okay?"

"I'm fine." She frowned. "I'm worried about you."

"What's going on?" Royce said, joining them.

"Who are you?" Sara said.

"Your attorney," Royce said. "Will hired me."

"Ambulance is here," Nate said.

Will stood, Sara holding onto one arm for support, while Nate gripped the other. He flopped down onto a stretcher, but wouldn't let go of Sara's hand.

"I need to—"

"Go find Petrellis," Sara interrupted Nate. "I'll ride with Will."

As Will was being examined by medical staff, he worried what his in-laws would think, what they would say. This would be the second time he'd been examined by doctors at the hospital in the past few days. In Mary's and Ed's minds, he probably threw himself onto the path of danger yet again by interacting with a suspected…what? What was Officer Petrellis, exactly? Will still didn't know.

Once they reached the hospital, Will was given a medication to counteract the drug. His brain fog began to clear and he was able to focus again. Sara said she'd be in the waiting room speaking with Royce, who had followed them from the police station.

Will puzzled over Nate's sudden turnaround from almost arresting her to letting her accompany Will to the hospital.

"How's your vision?" the nurse asked.

"Good, excellent," Will answered.

"Are you nauseous or dizzy?"

"No, ma'am. I'm much better now, thanks. Can I go?"

"Where's the fire?" Dr. Kyle Spencer, a member of SAR asked, coming into the ER. "Hey, buddy, I heard you were brought in."

"Hey, Spence," Will said.

"How's the head?"

"Fine."

"No headache?"

"No."

"Blurred vision?"

"Not now."

"So…when?" Spence studied him with concern.

"After I got stuck with the drug."

Spence pulled out a penlight and checked Will's eyes. "Did you fall and hit your head again?"

"Not that I know of."

Spence was referring to an altercation in the mountains last year. That injury had left Will with temporary, selective amnesia. At the time Will didn't remember that Megan had passed away. Once his memory returned, reliving that grief had left him gutted, as if she'd just died.

"The medical team identified elements of the drug we

found in Spike's system and were able to give him, and now you, something to counteract the effects," Spence said.

"Yeah, so they told me."

"It wouldn't hurt to rest this afternoon."

"Okay, doc." Will shifted off the gurney and planted his feet on the floor.

Spence studied him. "A-OK?"

"Solid as a rock, thanks."

"Excellent." They shook hands. "Until our next mission, then."

"Yep." Will left the examining room and found Sara in the waiting area with Royce.

"Hey, how are you?" Sara went in for a hug.

It was a brief embrace that shocked Will. He didn't want to let go.

"I'm okay," Will said. "Was Royce able to help you?"

"Turns out it wasn't necessary," Royce said. "In case you do need me, you've got my card." Royce smiled at Will. "Glad you're okay. Take care."

"You, too."

Royce left the ER waiting area and that was when Will noticed a uniformed officer by the door.

"Okay, someone's going to have to draw me a map here," Will started. "This morning Nate was arresting you, then he did a one-eighty and let you accompany me in the ambulance and now he's posted a police officer, I'm assuming for your protection?"

"Yeah, you and I need to talk. It's rather crowded here. Officer Carrington will take us to the station, unless you need to go home and rest?"

"No, I'm okay."

Will and Sara left the hospital with Officer Carrington, Sara's eyes constantly scanning their surroundings. She seemed different today, stronger, more sure of herself.

He almost wondered if she was the same person he'd

found in the mountains. Of course she was, yet something had definitely changed.

And he liked it, especially the hugging part.

The ride back to the station was somewhat quiet. Will was desperate to know what was going on, but didn't dare ask in front of a third party.

Officer Carrington escorted them into a conference room at the station. Sara wandered to the window and looked outside.

"First, I need to apologize for bringing this danger to Echo Mountain—" she turned "—and into your life."

"I don't see a need to apologize. Go on." He pulled out a chair at the table and sat, hoping she'd join him. She leaned against the wall and crossed her arms over her chest.

"The truth is, I'm FBI. I was on an undercover mission to find evidence against a company called LHP, Inc.—LaRouche, Harrington and Price's company. I suspect they plan to distribute a sleep medication that will make them millions, and potentially put lives at risk."

"You followed them on a hiking trip?"

"I bought my way onto the guide team, hoping they'd let their guard down and I'd find evidence of their plan. Then I saw Vic LaRouche throw David Price to his death. Wasn't expecting that."

"Have you told Nate this?"

"This morning, when he picked me up. He kind of—" she hesitated "—guilted it out of me."

"Yeah, I could see him doing that."

"Now I feel even more guilty because of what happened to you this afternoon."

"You didn't stick me with the drug."

"Don't be so literal here, Will. This is my fault. Maybe if I would have made a different choice."

"What choice? You've been in survival mode ever since you witnessed the murder."

She cocked her head slightly. "How do you do that?"

"What?"

"Offer so much compassion for someone who has been making your life a mess."

"What mess? I don't see a mess."

"Will, Petrellis knows you and I are connected, so now you're a target. The smartest thing for me to do is leave town and somehow draw them away from Echo Mountain."

"Why did Nate take you in this morning?"

She pulled out a chair and sat at the table. Good, she was getting closer.

"LaRouche and Harrington reported David Price missing this morning," she said. "They claim he disappeared after he and I got into an argument."

"So they're turning this around on you?"

"Looks that way."

"But you're FBI."

"They don't know that, and they can't." She reached across the table and placed her hand on Will's. "Only you and Nate know who I really am," she said. "It has to stay that way. If these guys find out the FBI is on their trail, they'll bury evidence so deep we'll never find it."

His gaze drifted to her hand, and she slid it off.

"You seem different," he said, glancing into her eyes. "More grounded and confident."

"It feels better to have people know the truth, people I trust." She cracked a slight smile.

The door opened and Nate joined them wearing a frown. He planted his hand on Will's shoulder. "Doing okay?"

"Yeah, I'm good. How's Spike?"

"Embarrassed, but otherwise good."

"And Petrellis?" Sara said.

"In the wind. For now."

"What's his motivation?" she asked Nate.

"Have no clue. Yet."

"Why did he take early retirement?" she said.

"He had issues at home and it interfered with his work."

"What kind of issues?"

"Not sure. He was a private guy." Nate slapped a folder onto the table. "We've got a bigger problem."

Will and Sara shared a worried look.

"One, your investigation has made Will a target," Nate said.

"Hey, Nate—"

Nate put up his hand to silence Will. "And, two, according to your supervisor, there is no case. Officially, you're on vacation, so that makes you a rogue agent with a vendetta."

TEN

"That's not true," Sara said, her face heating with anger. Why couldn't Bonner support her and admit she had been working on a case?

"Sara, what's going on?" Will said with a puzzled frown.

"It's easy, Will," Nate said. "Your friend here has been lying to us and manipulating us this whole time."

Will studied her with such pain in his eyes. "You've been lying to me?"

Regret coursed through her. No, she had good intentions, even if her execution was off.

"Will." She leaned forward. "I'm sorry, truly. But I'm doing the right thing here. My boss probably threw me under the bus because he's tired of me hounding him about tough cases, the criminals that get away." She glanced over her shoulder at Nate. "You worked in a big city—you know what I'm talking about."

Nate didn't answer, so she continued, redirecting her attention to Will, wanting him to know everything.

"LaRouche and Harrington were trying to convince David Price to go along with their plan to distribute a dangerous drug that could kill people. Because of who they are and their influence and who knows what else, they're going to get away with it. That's why LaRouche shoved David Price off the cliff—because he was going to walk away from the company, which would have raised suspicion and tanked their stock. So yes, I came out here because I didn't have enough evidence, and I decided to find more. Call me nuts, call me rogue, I don't care, as long as I put these guys away before they kill anybody." She glanced at Nate once more. "Didn't you ever watch a suspect walk away with a cocky smirk on his face when he should have been in cuffs?"

Nate tapped a pen against his open palm and studied her. "How do you know the drug is dangerous?"

At least he was listening to her. Now if she could get Will to forgive her for lying.

"They were arguing about an anomaly in the test results," she explained to Nate. "David Price said it wasn't right, that it could kill people. I recorded it on my phone, which was damaged in my fall. I was hoping a tech could still retrieve the video. That's my nail in their coffin."

"What motivated you to follow them into the mountains?" Nate asked.

"An email exchange between LaRouche and the drug testing company. I printed them out. My supervisor said it wasn't enough."

"Why not?" Nate said.

"It was too—" she made quote marks with her fingers "—vague."

She glanced at Will, who still looked like a man who'd just met her for the first time. As if he didn't recognize her. Shame burned her insides, both for having lied to him, and for putting him in danger.

She shifted in her chair and waited for more questions from Nate.

"He said once you got your teeth into something, you weren't giving it up," Nate said. "Even if there was no basis for an investigation."

"Nice," she muttered.

"He told you to let this one go," Nate continued.

"Well, I couldn't."

"You ignored a direct order."

"He ordered me to take vacation time—"

"Because you hadn't taken time off in five years."

"I didn't have any reason to."

"But you had reason to go against a direct order and pursue this case?"

"If it could save lives, yes," she countered. "I can't believe you've never done the same."

"We're not talking about me. We're talking about you, and why you're so tenacious. Your boss said—"

"What, that I'm an aggressive head case because I hid in a closet while a random home invader broke in, killed my father and made me and my little brother orphans? As if we hadn't been through enough after Mom died."

Sara shook her head in frustration and stared at the gray laminate table. Silence filled the room. There, she'd said it, what everyone who knew her, and knew about her past, thought whenever she did anything off book.

Someone knocked on the door and a secretary poked her head inside. "The chief wants to see you, Nate. It's important."

"I'll be right back." Nate followed the secretary out of the room and shut the door, leaving Sara and Will alone.

With her shame spread out on the table, exposed for him to see.

She clenched her jaw, wishing she could be anywhere else, be anyone else at this moment. Will's opinion of her mattered more than it should.

"Sara?" he said.

She couldn't look at him. He pushed back his chair and came to her side of the table. He knelt beside her, reached for one of her hands and gently clasped it between his.

"I am so sorry about your father," he said.

She nodded.

"How old were you?"

"Twelve."

"Oh, honey." He pulled her against his chest and stroked her back.

She almost started crying and stopped herself. It would

only prove that they were right about her: that she was weak and fragile, and had no business in law enforcement.

"Don't." She pushed away and stood, pacing to the opposite side of the room. "I appreciate your compassion, but it only makes me feel worse."

"Why?"

She hesitated. Never in her life had she confided in anyone about Dad's death, not even her uncle. Right now, in this conference room, she ached to talk about it with Will. He wouldn't think her weak or damaged, would he? Knowing Will, he'd offer to hug her again.

She'd gone a lot of years without hugs. Maybe she should appreciate them while she could. Besides, once this case was done she'd leave town and never see Will again, never see the look of pity on his face because he knew the truth about Sara failing her dad.

"I guess," she started, "I don't deserve your compassion."

"Don't say that."

"Why not? I lied to you."

"You thought you were doing the right thing."

"Oh, Will. I'm not worthy of your compassion. I failed Dad and I keep failing victims who depend on me to protect them."

He took a few steps closer. "What victims?"

"People like the Williamsons, whose daughter was killed by members of a drug gang. She went missing and we were called in to find her. I was this close." She pinched her fingers. "Bonner, my supervisor, took me off the case. He said we'd invested too many man-hours in the investigation. Local police in Detroit found the girl's dead body a week later. I could have found her, Will. I know I could have."

"I'm sorry," he said.

"Yeah, well, sorry is for losers." She snapped her attention to him, afraid she'd hurt his feelings again. Surprisingly, he shared a look of understanding.

"No," he said. "Being sorry is a way to share a friend's burden. I'd like to share yours."

"Why?"

"I feel as if we've become friends. I wish you'd stop trying to push me away."

"But I lied to you about who I was."

"Because you were working a case. I get it, even if I'm disappointed that you felt you couldn't completely trust me."

"Stop being nice to me."

Will leaned against the wall and crossed his arms over his chest. The corner of his mouth turned up in a slight smile. "That's the second time you've said that. Now it's my turn to counter—toss that chip off your shoulder and get on with your life."

"What life?" she muttered.

"So it's really all about work for you?" Will said.

"You wouldn't understand. You have a family."

"And friends, and a church community," he added.

"Rub it in, why don't ya," she said teasingly.

He didn't smile. "My point is, there are many dimensions to life, not just work or family. Maybe, while you're in Echo Mountain, you could experience some of those other things."

"My goal is to not only nail LaRouche and Harrington, but also to keep my distance from people so I don't put them in jeopardy."

People, meaning Will. From the disappointed look on his face, he obviously got the message.

The door popped open and Nate came into the room. "I spoke with our chief. We think it best if you stay undercover for the time being to continue the investigation of LaRouche and Harrington."

"You believe me?"

"Yes, I do," Nate said. "Although I don't appreciate you lying to me. The chief and I also realize we have a bigger problem." He looked at Will. "You've become a target, my friend."

"Because Petrellis came after me?" Will said. "No, I happened to be at the wrong place at the wrong time. That's all."

"Let's assume Petrellis is working for LaRouche and Harrington, that they hired him to find Sara, find out what she told authorities. He knows the two of you are connected, which means he can get to her through you. And possibly get to you through your girls."

Sara's heart ached. She'd done this. She'd dragged two adorable little girls into the ugliness of her work.

"Will, I'm so—"

"What do you recommend, Nate?" He cut Sara off.

"We'll put police protection on the house tonight while we look for a place to relocate you and the girls," Nate said.

"Where to?" Will asked.

"How about the resort?"

"They were booked last time I checked," Will said.

"Maybe the resort's had some no-shows," Sara offered, trying to be both helpful and hopeful.

An emotion so foreign to her, yet she'd embrace hope if it might help the girls. Help Will.

"How about Bree's cottage at Echo Mountain Resort?" Nate suggested. "She's got an extra room upstairs, and a state-of-the-art security system. Plus, with everyone around for the festival, Petrellis wouldn't be foolish enough to try anything."

"I'd hate to impose on her like that," Will said.

"Come on, buddy, you know Bree. She'd be offended if we didn't ask for her help."

Will nodded. "True."

"Why don't you call her, Will?" Sara said.

"It's settled," Nate said. "You call Bree and I'll send Sara's phone to the lab in Seattle to see if they can pull the recording off it."

"How long will that take?" she said.

"Depends how backed up they are."

"Or we could take it to Zack Carter at the resort," Will said. "He's an amazing tech specialist."

"Can't. It's a chain of evidence thing," Nate explained. "I take it from Sara and it goes directly to the lab. Otherwise, once this goes to court they could challenge the third-party intervention."

"Oh, right," Will said.

Nate extended his hand for Sara's phone. She hesitated. "No offense, but this is not just a recording. It's my life."

"I understand," Nate said. "I'll make sure it gets into the right hands. I'll put a rush on it."

Will shot her an encouraging nod.

Sara handed Nate the phone, trying to process this new feeling—this feeling of genuine trust.

"I'll set up police protection for tonight," Nate said. "Tomorrow we'll covertly relocate you and the girls."

"We have church in the morning," Will said.

"I'll assign myself to that detail and keep watch outside. Sara, I'd advise you to stay in the loft until further notice."

"I can't do that."

"Excuse me?" Nate said.

"I'm responsible for Will and his girls being in danger. I want to be close enough that I can be part of your protective detail."

"Absolutely not," Nate said. "You're a trouble magnet."

"Nate," Will admonished.

Sara didn't let the comment affect her. "No one will know I'm there. I'll change my appearance, whatever is necessary, but I won't abandon Will and his girls."

"Even if that could prove dangerous for them?" Nate said.

"Then, we find Petrellis first. We'll use me as bait to catch him."

"Sara, no," Will said.

"I will not keep looking over my shoulder," Sara said. "And I certainly don't want him terrorizing your family, Will." She redirected her attention to Nate. "How about it?"

"Okay, let's get Will and the girls settled, then we'll cast a line for Petrellis."

"I wish you wouldn't do this," Will said to Sara.

"This is my job. On a normal day I'm pretty good at it."

"But you're hurt—"

"I'll be fine."

She'd do whatever was necessary to make sure Will and his girls were out of danger.

Sara sipped her hot tea as she sat at the counter in the town's most popular diner. It was a long shot, but the best plan they could come up with on short notice.

Nate waited outside with another officer in an unmarked car. The agreement was Sara would text them when Petrellis showed up. Surely someone in this crowded restaurant knew Petrellis, and many of them had heard of her—the strange woman who'd been rescued from the mountains. She could tell from their expressions, from their curious frowns as they passed by.

But somehow she was going to disguise herself when she joined the protective detail for Will and the girls? Who was she kidding? She was probably the town's biggest celebrity.

Which she hoped worked in her favor right now. Hopefully her diner visit would start a buzz about the mysterious lady who fell off the mountain and had been rescued by the local bachelor. Sara was under the impression locals were not only protective of Will, but also wanted to find him a suitable mate.

Sara was not at the top of that list, even on her best day. Will was about compassion and raising his girls in a healthy environment. Sara was about...well, you wouldn't call her lifestyle necessarily healthy.

For the first time in years, she caught a glimpse of her obsessive nature, a nature that turned people off, especially her superiors at work. And now she was so obsessed with keeping Will and his girls safe that she was putting herself in danger. Yeah, *obsessive* was a good word to describe her current decision. It was part of the job, a job Will would never truly understand.

The restaurant wall clock read nine fifteen. She wondered what Will was serving his girls for dinner. Probably something healthier than the cheeseburger and fries sitting on the counter in front of her. Would Will read Claire and Marissa a bedtime story? Work on their Christmas lists?

The waitress, a middle-aged woman with black hair pulled back, came by with a water pitcher. "How was the burger?"

"Good, thanks."

"Need more water?"

"No, I'm good."

"Can I ask you something? I mean, if I'm being rude just tell me."

"Go for it."

"Are you her? The woman who fell off the mountain and was rescued by Will Rankin?"

Success! Word had spread. They knew who she was.

"Yes, that's me."

"Where are you from?"

"Seattle."

"Ah, so hiking was a new experience for you."

Sara shrugged. She'd hiked plenty as a kid.

"Good thing Will happened to be out there," the waitress offered.

"Yep."

But not so good in Sara's book. Finding Sara had sent Will's life into a tailspin of trouble.

"Will's a nice man," the waitress said.

"Exceptionally nice."

"He's been through a lot."

"Yes, he has."

"So you know about his wife?"

"Yes, Will and I have become friends."

"Oh," she said, disappointed. A customer caught her eye and she walked away.

Sara's phone buzzed with a text. It was from Will.

You okay?

She responded.

All is well. How are the girls?

She glanced over her shoulder toward the door. The waitress stood beside a table of customers, three elderly couples who seemed to be glaring at Sara.

Oh, boy. Her friendship with Will was causing her to be the most disliked person in town. She redirected her attention to her phone. Will hadn't responded. She didn't want to look back at the locals in the corner. Their message was clear. "You should be ashamed of yourself for involving Will."

Oh, she was very ashamed of herself for putting him in danger. Yet, she kept hearing Will's voice: *I wish you'd stop trying to push me away.*

He appreciated their friendship, or whatever you could call what was developing between them. Every time she tried drawing a boundary line, he'd reach right across and hold on tighter. What kind of man did that?

A compassionate, generous man.

One who deserved better than a damaged friend like Sara Vaughn in his life.

The waitress returned and placed the check on the counter. A hint that Sara had overstayed her welcome?

"Thanks," Sara said.

With a nod, the waitress walked away. Sara flipped over the check, and noticed a message written in ink: "Meet me out back."

She scanned the restaurant. A few people still stared at

her, but chances were none of them had written the message. She placed cash in the bill sleeve and shifted off the barstool. Cradling her sprained wrist against her stomach, she went down the hall leading to the bathroom. At the end of the hall was a bright red exit sign over a back door.

This could be it. Either Petrellis waited outside for her, or it was a local wanting to give her a lecture about staying away from Will. She pulled out her phone to text Nate, and hesitated.

Once Petrellis was brought in for questioning, he'd clam up like his kind usually did, hiding behind his lawyer.

She couldn't let that happen.

Pocketing her phone, she pushed the door open. A gust of wind sent a chill across her shoulders.

"Hello?" she called down the dark alley.

Her voice echoed back at her. Anxiety skittered across her nerve endings.

She knew what she was doing, she told herself. She was a smart agent who was going to get information out of Petrellis.

Suddenly someone gripped her shoulders hard, and shoved her forward.

"You don't have to restrain me," she said. "It's not as if I'm in any shape to fight back."

He led her to his car and pushed her into the driver's seat, then across into the passenger seat. She hit the record button on her new phone, hoping maybe this time the evidence wouldn't be destroyed.

Aiming the gun at her chest with one hand, Petrellis started the car and pulled out of the alley.

"Where are we going?" she said.

"Someplace we can talk."

"About?"

"Who you really are."

She stilled. Did he know? Had her cover been blown?

He shot her a side-eye glare as he headed out of town.

"Because you're not some random trail assistant or you'd be terrified of this." He waved his gun. "But you're not. Which means you have experience with guns."

"I was taught to shoot as a kid."

"Let's cut to the truth. Who sent you and what did you hear out there in the mountains?"

"So they did hire you to find me."

"What are you after?" he demanded.

"It was a job, that's all."

"You killed David Price, why?"

Whoa, so LaRouche and Harrington were telling their own people that Sara had killed him?

"I didn't kill him. LaRouche did."

"Stop lying. I need the truth!"

"I told you the truth."

"No, you didn't, but you will."

He turned onto a farm road and hit the accelerator. The car sped up, the speedometer needle reaching sixty miles per hour.

"Why are you doing this?" she cried.

"I have nothing to lose. My life is over."

The car sped toward an abandoned barn in the distance. Faster. Faster.

"Slow down!"

"Either I get answers from you or we both die. Makes no difference to me."

ELEVEN

Great, Sara had been kidnapped by a man with a death wish? No, there was more to this.

"What have they got on you?" she said.

"Tell me who hired you!" he countered.

"Are they blackmailing you? What? I know you're a cop—"

"Not anymore I'm not."

"I heard you had to retire early because of family issues. Have they offered you money?"

He sped up. Seventy miles per hour.

"Okay! I'm FBI!" she cried.

He shot her a look of disbelief.

"LaRouche and Harrington are the enemy here, not me," she protested.

The flash of police lights lit the car from behind.

He eyed the rearview, then refocused on the barn in the distance.

"You might want to die, but don't be a coward and take me with you. And what about the people who will die because of a faulty drug?"

He looked at her again.

"They didn't tell you about that, did they?" she said.

His foot eased up on the gas.

"You were a cop, a good cop," she said. "Getting the bad guys is in your blood. Help me stop them."

"I can't."

"Then, don't stop me from putting them away!"

She was grasping at the wind, but she had to try to get through to him. As the sirens wailed louder behind them, her heartbeat pounded against her chest. She didn't want to die this way.

Use your training. Talk him down.

"Innocent people will die. Do you want to be remembered as a murderer by your family? Your wife and kids?"

An ironic chuckle escaped his lips. "My kids don't care about me."

Okay, she'd hit a nerve. She was getting through to him.

"I don't believe that. They're going to be devastated when their father dies and is branded a criminal. There's still a chance to save yourself, Petrellis. Help us nail these guys."

A tear trailed down his cheek.

"Remember why you put on your uniform in the first place," she continued. "I could really use your help here, Stuart," she said, remembering his first name from the file she'd read at the police station.

He eased his foot off the accelerator. The barn loomed in the distance. He pressed down on the brake. The car came to a stop.

"I'm sorry," he said, and started to raise his gun.

To his own head.

She lunged, wrestling the gun away.

It went off, shattering the front windshield. Officer McBride whipped open the driver's door and pulled Petrellis from the car. Nate opened Sara's door. She shoved the gun at him and stumbled away from the car, trying to catch her breath, trying not to throw up.

She'd almost been killed. Twice. First by the suicide crash into the barn, then when she'd disarmed him.

What was she thinking?

That she couldn't watch a man die because of criminal jerks LaRouche and Harrington.

"Take a deep breath," Nate said.

"I'm fine, I'm fine." Her face felt hot and cold at the same time.

"Why didn't you text me when you saw him?" Nate said.

"Didn't want him lawyering up."

"You could have—"

"Don't leave him alone. He's suicidal. He tried shooting himself in the head. They've got something on him, Nate. Find out what it is. I think he'll help us if you can destroy whatever they've got on him."

"Okay, okay, breathe. You're going to hyperventilate."

"How's Will? Is he okay?"

"He's fine. Let's get you out of here."

As Will fed the girls dinner, he tried to stay present and engaged in their stories about the museum, and their grandpa ordering monster hash for lunch.

Thoughts about what was happening with Sara's plan to draw out Officer Petrellis kept taunting him.

A few hours later, as he tucked them into bed, little Marissa asked, "Are you mad at us?"

Both girls looked at him with round green eyes.

"No, why would I be upset with you?" he said, glancing across the room at Claire.

"Because you've got that grandma look on your face," Claire said.

"What look?"

"You know, like this." Claire scrunched up her nose and pursed her lips in the patented grandma, disapproving frown.

Will smiled. "I look like that?"

Marissa nodded that he did.

"I'm sorry, girls. The fact is, I'm distracted because I'm worried about a friend."

"Miss Sara?" Claire asked.

"Yes. She's having a tough time and I think she could use a friend or two right about now."

"Doesn't she have any friends?" Marissa asked.

"I don't think so. She works so much and has no time for friends."

"That's sad," Claire said.

"But God's her friend," Marissa offered.

"Let's say a prayer for her." Claire climbed out of bed and kneeled, interlacing her fingers. Marissa followed suit, and Will's heart warmed. They were such good, loving girls.

He interlaced his fingers. "Who wants to lead?"

"I do, I do!" Marissa said.

The room quieted.

"Give us this day our daily bread—"

"Wrong one," Claire corrected.

"Oh, yeah." Marissa cleared her throat. "Dear God in Heaven, we are praying for our friend Miss Sara, who can't draw, and has no friends, but she's really nice and we like her anyway. We pray that she..." Marissa hesitated and looked at Will.

"Is safe," Will said.

"Is safe," the girls echoed.

"Is at peace," Will said.

"Is at peace."

"And will open her heart to the wonder of grace. Amen."

"Amen," the girls said.

"Okay, back into bed. I've got a surprise for you tomorrow after church."

"What kind of surprise?" Claire said.

"It wouldn't be a surprise if I told you." He tucked her in and kissed her forehead. "I think you're going to like it."

He went to Marissa's bed and tucked her in, as well.

"Love you, Daddy."

"Love you, pumpkin."

Will went to the door and switched off the light; the ceiling lit up with the twinkling of glow-in-the-dark stars.

He shut the door, appreciating the moment, realizing in a few years Claire wouldn't want to share a room with her little sister.

Will had plenty of work to catch up on, which he hoped would keep his mind off Sara. He fixed himself a cup of tea and went into the living room to enjoy the colorful lights on the Christmas tree while he worked.

He opened his laptop and forced himself to focus. One of his best clients, Master Printing, had had their website hacked and taken down by search engines. He'd rewritten the code and corrected the problem, so he signed on to check if their website was back online. There wasn't much an SEO specialist like Will could do to force the search engines to reupload the pages. Still, he let them know the situation had been rectified.

A soft knock sounded from the door. He wondered if he'd imagined it. He stood and peeked through the window. Sara stood there with Nate behind her.

Will opened the door. "Thank God you're okay."

Sara wrapped her arms around Will and squeezed. Tight.

"Let's go inside," Nate said, looking over his shoulder.

"Sorry," Sara said, releasing Will.

"Why? I was thinking of doing the same thing." He put his arm around her and led her to the sofa.

"Actually, could I use the bathroom?" Sara asked.

"Sure, at the end of the hall on the right," Will said, and offered a smile.

It looked as if Sara tried to smile, but couldn't get her lips to work. She disappeared around the corner.

"You got Petrellis?" Will asked Nate.

"We got him."

"You don't sound happy about it."

"She went rogue on me, Will," Nate said, frustration coloring his voice. "I told her to text me when she saw Petrellis. Instead, she got into his car, and he…" Nate shook his head.

"He what?" Will fisted his hand.

"He almost killed them both, then tried to shoot himself in front of her."

"Oh, Sara," he whispered.

"She disarmed him, but she shouldn't have been there in

the first place," Nate said, frustrated. "I apologize for bringing her here. She was insistent."

"No, it's okay," Will said. "I would have been up all night worrying about her anyway. At least I can see she's okay, sort of."

"The chief is trying to get Petrellis to work with us. The guy's pretty messed up. I guess his wife's in bad shape."

"How so?"

"She's got multiple sclerosis. Living in a nursing home in Bellingham, very expensive. LHP's security chief tracked Petrellis down and offered him a boatload of money to find Sara and figure out what she was up to. Petrellis needed the money to keep his wife in the Bellingham facility." Nate hesitated. "I had no idea she was so sick."

"How did LaRouche and Harrington track him down so quickly?"

"Companies like LHP employ top-notch IT specialists who probably went through bank records and personal histories to identify someone they could manipulate. I wonder who else they targeted in town."

"And no one knew about Petrellis's wife?"

"Nope. I feel bad about that. Why didn't he talk to the chief?"

"Sometimes if you don't talk about it, you can pretend it's not happening," Will offered, speaking from personal experience. "What I still don't understand is how LaRouche and Harrington discovered Sara was in Echo Mountain."

"The whole town knew she'd been rescued by SAR. Wouldn't be hard for them to figure it out."

"What happens next?"

"Waiting to hear from the chief," Nate said. "I still want to move you and the girls to the resort. Did you speak with Bree?"

"She graciously invited us to move into her cottage."

"And Aiden's holding a private room for Sara at the resort."

"So you'll set her up there, as well?"

"That's the plan, not that she'll take orders." Nate's phone buzzed.

"You get that. I'm going to check on Sara," Will said.

"Detective Walsh." Nate wandered to the front window.

As Will headed for the hall, he heard the echo of little girl voices.

"I like those the best," Marissa said.

"That's because they're little, like you," Claire said.

"You make that sound like a bad thing."

It was Sara's voice. Will hesitated, not wanting to interrupt the moment.

"She always teases me about being little," Marissa said.

"I was little when I was a kid," Sara offered.

"You were?" Marissa said.

"Yep. Sometimes kids made fun of me, but my dad used to call me his little darling, which made it all okay."

"Does he still call you that?" Claire asked.

Will took a step toward the bedroom, wanting to intervene.

"My dad's in Heaven," Sara said.

"With Mommy." Marissa hushed.

The room fell silent. Will stepped into the room and froze. Sara was lying on the floor between the girls' beds, her hands folded across her chest.

"Hey girls," Will said.

Marissa jackknifed in bed. "Sara was little, too, Daddy."

"No kidding?"

Sara sat up and hugged her knees to her chest. "Sorry, they spotted me when I was walking by and asked me to come say good-night."

"I'm glad they did."

"Will you be here tomorrow, Miss Sara?" Claire asked.

"Maybe. We'll see. I'd better go so you can get some sleep."

"Daddy has a surprise for us tomorrow." Marissa clapped her hands in excitement.

Sara reached for Will, and he extended his hand to help her up. When she stood, they were only inches apart.

"Be careful of the mistletoe in the hallway," Claire said in a singsong voice.

Marissa giggled.

"Okay, girls, bedtime. For real," Will said. He motioned Sara out of the room and shut the door so adult voices wouldn't disturb them.

"They're so..." Sara started. "Precious."

"You sure you don't mean precocious?"

She stopped in the hallway, inches from the dreaded mistletoe, and placed an open palm against his chest.

"You're right, you are so—" she hesitated as if she struggled to form the word "—blessed."

In that moment, everything seemed to disappear: the danger, his anxiety about his in-laws and the fact that his best friend stood in the next room.

Will leaned forward and kissed Sara on the lips—a brief, loving kiss.

When he pulled back, her blue eyes widened and she pressed her fingertips to her lips.

Giggling echoed behind him. He turned and spotted his girls watching from a crack in their door.

"Bed," he ordered.

They slammed the door. When he turned around, Sara was walking into the living room.

Will sighed. Had he upset her?

He followed her into the living room where Nate continued his phone call.

Will sat next to Sara on the couch. She studied her fingers in her lap.

"So...am I in trouble?" Will asked.

She snapped her gaze to meet his. "No, but I am."

He studied her blue eyes, trying to discern the meaning

of her words. Had something happened with the case, or was she referring to the kiss? Did she share the strong feelings he was developing for her, and decided that was unprofessional?

"Okay, I'll figure it out. Thanks, Chief." Nate ended his call and turned to Will and Sara. "Petrellis has been medicated for now. He went nuts on the way to lockup and they rushed him to the hospital. The chief likes our plan about relocating you at the resort, but suggested Sara head back to the station with me and spend the night in a cell."

"Nate, come on, why can't she stay at the loft?" Will said. "No one knows about it."

"The station is harder to breach, plus someone is always there. I can't put twenty-four-hour guard on both your house and the loft."

"Then, let Sara stay here, at the house."

"Will—"

"My home office doubles as a guest room." He interrupted Sara's protest, and looked at Nate. "You've got us under police protection anyway. This makes the most sense."

"Not to me, it doesn't," Sara said.

Nate sighed. "He's got a point. Keeping you all in one spot will make our job easier. I'll call the chief and let him know. I'll take the first shift. Better get my overnight bag from the truck." Nate went outside.

"I shouldn't be staying here, Will," Sara said.

"You don't belong in a jail cell." He stood and extended his hand. "Come on, I'll show you to your room."

She took his hand and he gently held on, anticipating her wanting to pull away.

She didn't.

He led her down the hallway and flipped on the light. Papers were scattered across the daybed.

"Sorry." He rushed over and collected them and then placed them on his desk. "The bed's only been slept in a few times, when Megan's sister came to visit. Clean towels are in the guest bathroom, which we rarely use. What else?" He looked around the room.

She reached out and touched his cheek. "Thank you."

"Of course."

"For so many things."

The walls felt as if they were closing in, and he could hardly breathe. Her gorgeous blue eyes studied him, as if she was trying to tell him something, something important, and intimate.

"Whatever happens, please know how much I appreciate you…" She hesitated. "Your generosity and your strength. You amaze me."

"My ego thanks you."

His gaze drifted to her lips. He wanted to kiss her again.

"I…I could use a glass of water," she said, her voice soft.

"We've got that here," he teased. "In the kitchen."

She didn't move. Neither did he.

Will's heart pounded against his chest. He sensed she needed to put distance between them, and he understood why. It was important they stayed focused on remaining safe, and not get distracted by their attraction to one another, or the promise of…did he dare say love?

Two loud cracks echoed from outside the window.

Followed by a crash.

And the house went dark.

TWELVE

Sara protectively yanked Will away from the window and pulled him into a crouch.

"Daddy! Daddy!" the girls cried.

"Go to the girls," Sara said calmly. "And stay down."

They both felt their way into the dark hallway.

"Where do you keep flashlights?" she asked.

"Everywhere. Kids are afraid of the dark. Got one in here." He opened a hall closet and fumbled for a second, then handed her a flashlight.

"What about you?"

A light winked from inside the girls' bedroom. "Claire's on it."

"Daddy!" Claire called.

"Go." Sara pointed the flashlight so he could make his way down the hall.

"You aren't going outside, are you?"

"No. Go on, they need you." She gave him a gentle shove. Once he was in the room with his girls, Sara went into the living room and peered through the curtain. The entire block was dark.

Neighbors opened their doors. She spotted a neighbor across the street starting down his front steps to investigate.

"What is going on?" she whispered.

She watched a few more neighbors wander outside, then head toward the end of the block. She went to another window to search the dark street. Someone flipped on their car headlights, illuminating a vehicle that had collided into an electrical pole. It must have damaged the transformer.

"Yikes." She wondered if the driver had been under the influence, or if he'd hit the gas instead of the brake by accident.

Another set of headlights clicked on, illuminating the street in front of Will's house. She snapped her attention to Nate's car and spotted someone kneeling beside Nate, who was on the ground.

"Oh, no," she said in a hushed tone.

She wanted to check on him, but figured he'd be furious if she left the house. She called 911, but they'd already been alerted about the accident and downed police officer.

"What happened?" Will said coming into the room.

Little Marissa dashed to Sara and wrapped her arms around her from behind. Tense from the past hour, Sara fought the urge to untangle the girl's arms from her waist. *Stop thinking about yourself and consider how much this little girl needs female comfort.*

"Looks as if a car hit the transformer," Sara said, stroking Marissa's hair. "Your neighbors are taking care of things."

"Can I see?" Claire said.

"No," Sara said.

Claire stopped dead in her tracks. Will looked at Sara in question.

"The car is pretty smashed up, and the driver is probably…" She hesitated. "Well, images like that can give you nightmares for weeks. Trust me, I've had my share of those."

"You have?" Marissa said, looking up at her.

"Yup. Better idea, let's light some candles and have a party."

"A party, cool." Claire started for the kitchen, where Sara assumed they kept the candles.

"Me, too," Marissa said, chasing after her sister.

As they rooted around in drawers, Sara motioned Will to come closer.

"Was it really a transformer?" he said in a soft voice.

"Yes, but there might be more to it. Nate is hurt."

"Where, outside?"

"Yes."

Will started for the front door. "I've gotta help him."

"Will, your girls—"

He whipped open the door just as Nate came stumbling into the house with help from Will's neighbor.

"I tried keeping him down until the ambulance came. He wasn't having any of it," the elderly neighbor said.

"What happened?" Will asked.

"I'm fine." Nate collapsed on the couch.

"I'm Sara," she said, extending her hand to the neighbor.

"Oscar Lewis, nice to meet you." They shook hands.

"Yay, more people for the party!" Marissa said, coming out of the kitchen.

Claire took one look at Nate and said, "What happened to Detective Nate?"

"Car clipped me," Nate said.

"Marissa, take the candles. I'll get some ice." Claire unloaded the candles into her sister's arms and disappeared into the kitchen. Sara marveled at how mature the eight-year-old Claire acted in the face of a crisis.

Sirens wailed from the street.

"Oscar, can you tell them I'm in here?" Nate said.

"Sure, police and EMTs?"

"I don't need an ambulance, but the driver of that sedan will."

Oscar left and Sara shut the door. Marissa stood in the corner, lining up candles.

"Hey, baby M, can you help your sister?" Will asked. "We need ice, and warm, wet towels for detective Nate's cuts and bruises."

"Okay, Daddy." Marissa danced off to join her sister in the kitchen.

Sara sat on a coffee table in front of Nate, Will hovering close by. "What really happened?" Sara said to Nate.

"I'm not totally sure. One minute I was texting, the next,

a sedan was speeding toward me. I dived out of the way, but he clipped me. I went down, shot at his back tire and he crashed."

"Why would he run you down?" Sara said.

Nate shook his head. "This case is getting stranger by the minute."

A knock sounded at the front door. Will went to open it.

A cute blond woman in her twenties rushed into the living room, spotted Nate and froze. "You're hurt."

"I'm fine," Nate said.

"I heard the call go out and came to see—"

"I'll answer questions for the blog tomorrow, Cassie. This isn't the time."

Sara read more than curiosity on Cassie's face. Sara read true concern.

And Nate was oblivious.

"What happened?" Cassie said, taking a step toward him.

Claire rushed into the room carrying an ice bag wrapped in a towel. "Here's the ice."

"He needs ice?" Cassie said.

"Where do you need it?" Claire asked.

"My knee would be great."

Claire held the ice pack to his knee, and an odd expression crossed Nate's face. "You'll probably get a better story by interviewing the neighbors."

"Really?" Cassie said, her voice laced with sarcasm. Shaking her head, she muttered, "Turkey." She stormed out of the house.

Sara and Will shared a look.

"I saw that," Nate said.

"Who was she?" Sara asked.

"She writes a community blog. I'm her source."

"Yeah, that's one word for it," Will said.

"Focus, guys," Nate said. "Obviously you're not safe here."

"Not a problem," Will said. "I'll call Bree and we'll head over there tonight."

"Head where, Daddy?" Claire said.

"Echo Mountain Resort. We're going to stay there for a while."

Another knock sounded at the door and Will answered. Chief Washburn joined them in the living room. "You okay?" he asked Nate.

"Yeah, but seriously frustrated."

"Well, you're gonna be more frustrated," the chief said. "The driver ran off."

"How is that possible?" Nate said.

"Neighbors saw where he headed. We'll do a search."

"Unbelievable," Nate said. "We lost another one."

"Let's focus on what we do have control over," Will said. "I'll help the girls pack."

Will and the girls were situated at Bree's cottage and fast asleep a few hours later. The girls shared an upstairs bedroom. Sara decided to stay upstairs as well, wanting to be close to protect Will, Claire and Marissa. Will and Nate bunked in the living room for the night.

Even with all the excitement, the girls were up bright and early the next day, ready for church. He asked them to be as quiet as possible so as not to wake Sara, yet she came down for breakfast. Will invited her to church, but she said she needed to focus on changing her looks. He suspected something else kept her from surrendering her troubles to God. That was a discussion for another time.

Officer Ryan McBride escorted Will and the girls to church, and stood guard outside. Nate hung back at the cottage to help Sara and brainstorm angles about the case.

During the service, Will said an extra prayer of thanks that Nate wasn't seriously injured last night.

The theme of the service was having faith during troubling times. Will embraced the message, needing the extra encouragement. He held firm to his faith regarding his abilities to be a good father, and he had faith things would work out for Sara.

Maybe even for Sara and Will?

From a practical standpoint, this relationship wasn't real. It was formed by tense emotions during dangerous circumstances. Sometimes love and practicality had little to do with one another. He was drawn to Sara, without question. Hopefully, after her case was solved, he could share his feelings. To what end? Her job, her life, was back in Seattle; sure, only three hours away, but it might as well be three thousand miles away. The next woman he married would have to be a good mom for the girls. Parenting wasn't a part-time job.

Parenting? Marriage? Between the excitement of yesterday and his clients' needs, Will was obviously sleep deprived, apparent in his random thoughts today.

"Go in peace and serve the Lord," Pastor Charles said. "Amen."

"Amen," the congregation repeated.

Will helped the girls on with their jackets, and waited while they buttoned up. Friends smiled and greeted him as they passed down the center aisle. Will offered greetings in return, exchanging pleasantries and a brief story or two.

With his girls on either side of him, Will clung to their hands and they made their way toward the exit. Once outside, he spotted Nate. Beside Nate stood a blond woman wearing a red ski cap and sunglasses. She looked like a teenager, and it took him a minute to realize it was Sara. She certainly had changed her looks.

Will led the girls toward Nate and Sara.

"You guys ready to head back to the resort?" Nate said.

"Yeah, they have an indoor pool," Claire said.

"Who's got a pool?" Will's mother-in-law, Mary, said over his shoulder.

"The resort," Claire said.

"Will, may I have a word with you?" Mary said.

"Sure, Mary, what's up?"

"Over here, please." She motioned for Will to join her a few feet away, while his father-in-law entertained the girls with a story.

"Mary?" he questioned.

She stopped, turned around and waved an envelope between them. "It's our official request for custody of the girls."

Will's heart dropped to his knees. "I don't understand."

"I haven't filed these papers, and I won't. Unless you continue to put the girls in harm's way."

"I would never—"

"You're not thinking straight, Will. I heard about last night, about how someone tried to run down Detective Walsh in front of your house. Why was the detective there anyway? Because he was keeping watch over the woman you rescued. Why was she at your house?"

"She was checking to see if I was okay."

"Why wouldn't you be okay?"

He didn't answer.

"Because something else happened that I don't know about." Mary sighed. "I stopped by the house last night and you and the girls were gone. Where did you stay?"

"At the resort."

"In hotel rooms?"

"No, at a friend's cottage."

"Because you were too frightened to stay in your own home. Do you see why I'm concerned?"

"We've got it under control."

"Look—" she hesitated "—you and I often don't see things the same way, but we agree on one thing, and that's the welfare of your girls."

"And?"

"Whatever trouble this woman is in, she's brought it into your life, correct?"

He didn't answer, he couldn't answer. She was right.

"I don't want a court battle, and I don't want to upset

Claire and Marissa, but I can't stand the thought of them being put in harm's way because you played the Good Samaritan."

He couldn't believe she was making him feel ashamed about helping a person in trouble.

"Let the girls stay with us until this situation is resolved, and we'll forget about this." Mary slipped the envelope into her purse.

"Will? Everything all right?" Sara said, approaching them.

His mother-in-law narrowed her eyes at Sara, and then glanced at Will. "Please call me by the end of the day and let me know your decision." She passed by Sara and motioned to Ed that they were leaving.

"What was that about?" Sara said.

"She's worried about the girls." He gazed across the parking lot at his daughters, under the protective eye of both Nate and Officer McBride.

"Because of me and the case," Sara said in a flat tone.

"Mary came to the house last night after hearing about the accident. We were gone. She figured out we didn't feel safe at the house. She threatened to take the girls away."

Sara touched his arm. "Will, no."

"Threatened, but she won't. She loves them too much. It would crush them to have us embroiled in a court battle over their welfare."

Marissa started to run off and visit with her friend Addy. Nate blocked her and shifted her closer to the car.

In that moment, looking at his baby girl's disappointed frown as she waved goodbye to her friend, Will realized this was no way for the girls to live—under the watchful eye of an overprotective father and police officers—until the case was solved and Will was out of danger.

It would break his heart to be away from them again, but he had to think of their well-being over his emotional needs.

"I need to talk to Nate."

As he headed toward Nate, Sara walked beside him. "You're a good dad," she said. "Don't ever forget that."

"Thanks." Will nodded at Nate. "Got a sec?"

Sara asked Claire a question about drawing, and both girls offered their advice. Will pulled Nate aside. "I'm thinking it might be easier on all of us, and safer for the girls, if they went away for a few days with their grandparents."

"Are you sure?"

"Yes. I should have suggested it sooner, but was missing them something fierce when I got home from my hiking trip."

"Setting them up at the resort—"

"Doesn't remove them from the potential danger. How safe do you think they'd be with my in-laws?"

"Safer than staying with you, especially if they take them out of town. Also, we could ask Harvey to tag along and play bodyguard. His cop instincts are razor sharp and he's got plenty of time on his hands since he retired from the resort."

"Good idea, thanks." Will gazed at his adorable girls. "I did the right thing by helping Sara, and now I have to do the right thing by keeping Claire and Marissa safe."

"Your in-laws might still be here." Nate craned his neck.

"No, not yet. I want to spend the day with the girls, then if you don't mind, could you take them over to Mary and Ed's?"

"Sounds good. Let's get you back to the resort."

Sara, Will and the girls hung out in Breanna McBride's cottage, drawing, baking and playing games. Sara had tried to isolate herself upstairs in the bedroom, but the girls were having none of it. They demanded she come downstairs and *visit*, as Marissa put it.

They made Christmas cookies, drank hot cocoa and laughed at silly jokes. Sara couldn't remember the last time she'd felt like a part of a family. Then Will told the girls his surprise was that Claire and Marissa were going on an adventure with their grandparents for a few days.

They were excited at first, then disappointed when they found out Will wasn't going. They moaned about missing their dad, and Sara's family moment shattered before her eyes. Rather than blame herself for the situation, Sara was more motivated than ever to wrap up this case so Will could get back to his life, his family.

And Sara could get back to…what?

She wasn't sure anymore. Was there even a job waiting for her back at the bureau? She didn't know. Oddly, she felt resentment toward her job. All of her determination, all of her drive to get the bad guys, had caused Will and his girls to be in danger, and now to be split up for their own protection.

The girls packed their things shortly after dinner and brought their bags down into the main entryway of the cottage.

"You just got home," Claire complained, hugging Will.

Sara looked away, the child's voice ripping at her heart. Marissa watched her big sister's reaction with curiosity, as if she was deciding if she was supposed to complain, as well.

"You girls are going to have fun with Nanny and Papa, okay?" he said to Claire.

"Okay," Claire said. "But no more adventures without you."

Marissa wrapped her arms around Sara's legs. "Bye, Sara."

"Bye, sweetie." She stroked the little girl's hair.

"Practice your drawing," Claire said. She looked at her dad. "Make sure she practices."

Will smiled. "Come on, I'll walk you girls to the car," he said, his voice raspy. "I'll be right back." Will nodded at Sara and escorted his girls out front.

Frustration burned low, and Sara marched into the kitchen. She started to pour herself a cup of coffee. Probably not a good idea to have caffeine at night, then again she wouldn't be able to get much sleep anyway, not until she could guarantee the safety of Will and the girls by putting LaRouche and Harrington away.

How was she going to do that? She wasn't even involved with the investigation, other than being a witness to the murder of David Price. She should be tracking down leads, helping Nate somehow, instead of baking cookies and playing board games with the girls.

She eyed the Christmas cookies, spread out on cooling racks. Little girls' laughter echoed in her mind as her gaze landed on a snowman cookie with green candy eyes and a red nose. Marissa had giggled uncontrollably when her dad had sprinkled powdered sugar on the cookie and called him Rudolph Frosty.

Sara wandered across the kitchen to the cookies and tried remembering a time when she'd made cookies with her dad, yet there was no memory of making Christmas cookies or telling jokes. Sara, her dad and Kenny had seemed to live under a cloud after her mom had randomly gotten sick and died.

"Shake it off," Sara scolded herself.

She left the kitchen and decided to check email in the living room. As she adjusted herself at Breanna's desk, she glanced out the window and spotted Will saying goodbye to the girls. He gave them each a big hug, and had to pry Claire's arms loose from his neck. A ball lodged in Sara's throat.

The girls finally got in the squad car and Will shut the door. When he turned, she saw him swipe at his eyes, and she felt even worse about dragging him into this mess.

There had to be a way to make it up to him.

Sure there was. Remove the threat. She reconsidered distancing herself from him, only they'd established that it wouldn't make a difference. They could get to Sara through Will.

Somehow word had gotten back to LaRouche and Harrington that Sara and Will had grown close, or maybe they knew that he'd saved her life and vice versa. Whatever the case may be, the only way to keep Will safe was to prove LaRouche and Harrington were the criminals she knew them to be: men who didn't care about killing innocent people for profit.

She refocused on the computer and checked her email. One caught her eye, an email from her boss demanding she call him ASAP. She pulled out her phone and called his cell. It went into voice mail.

"It's Agent Vaughn returning your call. The local police are being very helpful. I look forward to speaking with you." She ended the call, not feeling all that grateful to the man who didn't support her quest to nail LaRouche and Harrington, the man who insinuated to Nate that she'd lost her perspective and maybe, even, was off the rails.

"Bonner," she muttered, and paced the living room. Why did he have to make things so hard? Why didn't he believe her when she showed him the proof of tampering with test results?

This train of thought wasn't going to help her move forward. She'd been stuck in the past on so many levels, that it had almost become habit for her: dig her heels in and hold on like a pit bull with its teeth around an intruder's leg.

She made a mental list of things to discuss with Nate once he returned. In the meantime, the least she could do was be there to support Will. He must feel horrible about separating from his girls again. She wondered what was taking him so long to come back inside.

She went to the front door and hesitated before opening it. Would she find him crying on the front porch? She wasn't sure if she could handle that, nor could she handle the look of resentment in his eyes—resentment toward Sara for causing his life to be turned upside down and sideways.

A car door slammed outside. Nate had already left to take the girls to their grandparents' house, so it couldn't be his car. She opened the door and spotted Officer Carrington headed for the cottage. She scanned the area for Will.

"Wait, did Will end up going with the girls?" she asked, partly hopeful and partly disappointed.

"No, ma'am."

Her heart raced up into her throat. "Then, where is he?"

THIRTEEN

"Will!" Sara called out. She rushed past Officer Carrington to get a better look at the property.

"Ma'am, please get back in the house where it's safe."

"Not until we find him. Will!"

What could have happened? In those few minutes while Sara had been away from the window feeling sorry for herself, had another one of LaRouche and Harrington's men swung by and snatched Will?

"Ma'am, I insist you go inside where it's safe."

Of course, standing here in the open made her a target. If LaRouche and Harrington's men were using Will to lure her out, they had succeeded. She rushed past Officer Carrington, went back into the cottage and called Nate.

"Detective Walsh."

"It's Sara. Are you on speakerphone?"

"Yes."

"Call me after you drop off the girls." She ended the call. The last thing she wanted was to upset Claire and Marissa by announcing their father had gone missing.

She paced the kitchen and eyed the wall phone. Posted beside it was a list of numbers, including one that read Security. She used Bree's house line to call it.

"Hey, sweet Bree," a man's voice said. "I thought you were helping with the—"

"It's not Breanna. It's Sara, I'm staying in Bree's cottage. Who's this?"

"Scott Becket, security manager for the resort."

"Have you been briefed about my situation?" she asked.

"Yes, Nate told me you're undercover FBI. Is there a problem?"

"Will is missing," she said, trying to sound calm, but failing miserably.

"When did this happen?"

"A few minutes ago. He was saying goodbye to the girls, and then he was gone."

"I'm on it. Stay put."

The line went dead.

"Argh!" she cried. Sliding down the wall, she wrapped her arms around her bent knees, feeling utterly helpless. She buried her face in her arms, brainstorming a way to help them find Will without putting herself in danger.

Suddenly a wet nose nudged her ear. She looked up, and got a big, wet kiss on the cheek from Bree's golden retriever, Fiona.

"What's wrong?" Bree placed a bag of groceries on the kitchen table and kneeled beside Sara.

"It's Will" was all she could get out.

"What about him?"

"He's gone. I don't know where. He disappeared."

"I've got to call Scott."

"Already did."

"Good, then everything will be fine. Scott was an exceptional cop before becoming our security manager. Did you call Nate?"

"He's with the girls. He'll call after he drops them off."

"Then, there's only one thing left to do while we wait." Bree reached out and placed a comforting hand on Sara's shoulder.

And said a prayer.

Sara didn't fight it this time; she was so desperate for Will's safety that she bowed her head and opened her heart. She hoped that God was truly forgiving, that he'd hear Sara's heartfelt prayer and keep Will safe.

* * *

"Stop!" Will called.

He'd seen the man hovering on the grounds near the cottage, thanks to the resort's property lights, and Will had called out, demanding the stranger identify himself. Instead, he'd run.

And Will had taken off after him. Maybe not the smartest idea, but the burn of frustration had driven Will out into the night. Frustration about his girls being forced to go away with their grandparents, frustration about Sara being constantly threatened.

"What do you want?" Will called after the guy, who turned a corner. Great, a blind spot. What if he had a gun and was waiting for Will? He stopped and searched the ground for a weapon, a rock or tree branch, something.

This was not Will. He wasn't a violent man by nature.

Yet this stranger might have information to help the authorities with this case. Will couldn't let him get away. He'd do anything to help Nate prove Sara's innocence and the businessmen's culpability in the death of David Price.

He grabbed a rather large branch and hesitated before making the turn.

Took a deep breath.

And flung the branch around the corner. No reaction. Surely the man would have fired off a shot.

Will clicked on the flashlight app on his phone, took a deep breath and peered around the corner. He aimed the light up the trail. The man was gone. Vanished.

How was that possible? The trail took a sharp incline five hundred feet. There was no way the man would have made it to the top, and to the next switchback so quickly.

Then Will noticed something on the ground. He approached a discoloration and kneeled for a better look.

Fresh blood.

The man was wounded, which meant he wouldn't be able to fight very hard against Will once he caught up to him.

Will straightened and started up the trail, using the flashlight to scan left, then right. The blood trail led straight up, then disappeared.

Will pulled out his phone and called Nate.

"Where are you?" Nate said before Will could get off a greeting.

"Are the girls—"

"Just dropped them off. Sara said you disappeared. What happened?"

"I saw a man watching the house so I followed him."

"You what? Get back to the house."

"I'm on a trail leading from the back of the cottage into the mountains. The guy's hurt."

"You found him?"

"Not yet. I found fresh blood and—"

Something slammed against Will's shoulders and he went down, breaking his fall with his hands. He collapsed against the damp earth, the wind knocked from his lungs. The guy would have already shot him if he had a gun, so Will figured he'd stay down and pretend to be unconscious. Depending on how badly the stranger was hurt, Will could detain him until help arrived.

"I've got him," the man said into his phone. "You'll have to come get him. I'm injured."

By the time this man's associates came to get Will, Nate and the local police would be swarming the area. Good, then maybe they'd catch these guys and one of them would confess to working for LaRouche and Harrington.

"Aw, come on, that wasn't the deal," the guy argued.

Will cracked his eyes open and spotted the man's black military boots pacing back and forth. Will also spotted his phone a few inches away. Will snatched it.

The man, clearly agitated, didn't notice Will retrieving his phone. The assailant seemed anxious and frustrated, and definitely not on board with the orders coming from the other end of the phone.

"No, I never signed on for that.…Fine, I'll call my brother to help."

A few seconds of silence passed. Will figured they wanted his attacker to move Will's body. To where?

"Bobby, it's Jim. Get out here to Echo Mountain Resort, the trail behind Bree McBride's cottage. I've got a guy I have to keep hidden.…Will Rankin.…I know. I know! They threatened to tell the police about the morphine I stole from the hospital.…I had no choice. She's in a lot of pain.…You'd know if you bothered to stop by, big brother."

As the conversation continued, Will figured out that the criminal businessmen were blackmailing his assailant. Will suddenly remembered where he'd seen those boots before: at the hospital. This was Jim Banks, the security officer who'd helped them look for Sara.

Apparently LaRouche and Harrington were able to get to anyone in town.

"I can't go to jail!" Jim yelled at his brother on the phone.

He had paced a good twenty feet away, as if Jim didn't like to look at what he'd done to Will. Will took the opportunity to flip the situation around. He took a deep breath, stood and aimed the flashlight at his attacker.

"Jim?"

Jim spun around, whipped a knife out of his pocket and pointed it at Will with a trembling hand. Abrasions reddened his cheek, and his right jacket sleeve was soaked with blood.

"I have first-aid training," Will said. "I can help you."

"No, you can't. Come on." He flicked the knife sideways, motioning for Will to lead the way back down.

Which meant they'd be passing right by Bree's cottage. How could this guy think he'd get very far in public? The guy had obviously stopped thinking once he found himself working for LaRouche and Harrington.

Kind of like how Will had stopped thinking clearly when he'd taken off in pursuit of this man.

"I sense you don't want to do this," Will said.

"Stop the psychobabble and walk."

Will realized he'd had enough: enough of hiding out and enough being bullied. He was definitely done surrendering to violent situations without a fight. It was time to protect the people he cared about.

As he approached Jim, he glanced up ahead at the trail. "You're here!"

Jim instinctively looked to his right.

Will kicked Jim in the side and he fell to his knees. Will grabbed Jim's wrist and twisted until Jim let go of the knife. Will yanked Jim's arm behind his back and the man cried out in pain.

Will shoved him to the ground, pinning him with a knee to his back. "I don't want to hurt you."

Jim groaned in surrender.

"What happened to your arm?" Will said.

"Car accident."

"The accident outside my house last night?"

The guy nodded.

"Will!" Nate called.

Will spotted Nate and Scott jogging toward him, both wearing headlamps.

"How many guys?" Nate called.

"One guy. Jim Banks from the hospital," Will said.

"Found him," Scott said into his cell phone. "He's fine. We'll be back shortly."

"You've obviously got this under control." Nate raised a brow as he motioned for Will to move aside.

Will pushed off the guy, struggling to calm the adrenaline rush. Nate and Scott helped Jim up and he groaned.

"He's bleeding pretty badly," Will offered.

Nate and Scott looked at Will, as if shocked that Will had drawn blood.

"He was the driver who crashed into the pole last night," Will clarified.

"Whoa, okay. I was afraid you lost your temper," Nate said, then looked at Jim. "So what's this about?"

Jim studied the ground.

"Someone's blackmailing him," Will explained. "Something about stealing drugs from the hospital."

"Is that right?" Nate pressed, eyeing his suspect.

"Lawyer," Jim said.

"Sure thing. Right after we book you for attempted murder."

"What! I didn't attempt to kill anyone."

"Did he threaten you with a weapon?" Nate asked Will.

"A knife." He aimed his flashlight at the ground, and went to pick it up.

"I got it." Scott picked up the knife with gloved hands and analyzed it. "Yeah, this could definitely kill someone."

"No, that wasn't the plan. I needed him to come with me."

"Where?" Nate pushed.

"They said…they said to bring him to the water tower on the north side of town."

"For what purpose?" Nate asked.

"I don't know."

"Will!" Sara came racing around the corner, Officer Carrington right behind her.

"I'm sorry, sir," Carrington said to Nate. "Once she heard you'd secured the scene, I couldn't get her to stay put."

"How did she—"

"I called Bree," Scott interrupted Nate.

Sara spotted the knife in Scott's hand and snapped her gaze to Will. Her eyes widened with horror.

"I'm fine," Will said.

"He didn't…"

"He didn't. Let's go." He reached out for her and she hesitated, then took his hand. He didn't like her hesitation, wondering what was behind it.

They headed back down the trail toward the cottage, where two more squad cars were parked.

"Officer Carrington, take Will and Sara inside and keep them there," Nate said. "I'll swing by the hospital with Jim for medical attention." Nate put Jim in the backseat of a patrol car, and pointed at Will and Sara. "Stay inside, hear me?"

"Yes," Will said.

Bree bolted out of the house, her dog right beside her. The golden retriever rushed up to Scott.

"It's okay, girl. We're all okay." Scott scanned the property with a concerned frown, then forced a smile when he looked at Bree. "Let's get inside before Nate locks us up for disobeying orders."

Sara released Will's hand. He wasn't going to let her push him away. He cared about her. A lot.

Will put his arm around Sara's shoulder and pulled her close, whispering in her ear, "Don't push me away."

She shook her head in frustration.

Once they got into the cottage, Bree and Scott headed for the kitchen. "I've got cookies," Bree announced.

"We'll join you in a minute," Will said, leading Sara into a secluded corner of the living room.

He motioned her to a Queen Anne chair, and he shifted onto the footstool in front of her. Her gaze drifted to the hardwood floor.

"What's going on?" He tipped her chin to look at him.

"You could have been killed."

He took her hands in his. "Hey, you didn't make me follow Jim up the trail. That was my decision."

"I'm always involving people in my violent life and they get hurt and I can't seem to fix anything."

"Hold on a second. This isn't about what just happened, is it?"

She didn't answer, but she didn't pull her hands from his, so he pressed on.

"This is about your father?"

Silence stretched between them.

"Sara, you didn't do anything wrong, and you were certainly not responsible for what happened to him. He made the decision to protect you by hiding you in the closet."

Her gaze held his, her eyes tearing. "Why? Why did he do that?"

Will pulled her into a hug and stroked her back. "Because he loved you so very much. It's hard to understand until you have children of your own. You'd literally jump in front of a moving bus to save them. Your dad hid you in a closet so that you would live, and become this strong, tenacious woman who fights for justice."

She sighed against him. "You make that sound like a good thing."

"It *is* a good thing. Think of all the people you've protected. You have sacrificed your life, your happiness to fight for those who can't defend themselves because they're either ignorant of the danger, or don't have the skills to stop the violence. You've become a strong, dedicated woman thanks to your life experiences. God has been watching out for you, Sara, watching you choose the tough cases and fight the hard battles. Embrace what you are instead of thinking it should be different or somehow better. This is better. Here, being here with me."

"You should be holding on to your girls."

"I will, once we resolve this case and everyone is safe. I ache for them, sure, yet as a father I must sacrifice my own needs for theirs. So we're a lot alike, you and I, which is probably why we've connected this way." He continued to stroke her back, liking how it felt when she leaned into him, almost as if…

She needed him.

"I…I don't know what *this* is," she said.

"You don't have to define it, but answer me this. How do you feel, in this moment, here with me?"

"At peace, maybe even…blessed."

"Hold on to that and have faith the rest will work itself out."

* * *

Faith. Sara was pretty sure she'd given up on having faith a long time ago. She went to sleep that night with a curious sense of peace, dreaming about possibilities for the future. She'd never really thought about the future before, at least not beyond the next few weeks anyway.

Somehow, through the crises of the past few days, something had awakened inside of her, something akin to hope. Did she dare embrace it?

They had set Will up in a private apartment at the resort for the night, while Sara stayed in Bree's cottage. The resort's security manager, who was Bree's boyfriend, Scott, and Officer Carrington took turns keeping watch over the cottage. They parked two squad cars out front, the strategy being that the police presence would discourage another direct attack.

Sara hated feeling helpless to resolve this situation—her mess of a case—and still felt utterly responsible for bringing the danger to this charming town.

For bringing the danger into Will's life.

Today she would dedicate herself to helping the local authorities with their investigation any way she could.

She went downstairs and spotted Officer Carrington napping on the sofa, while Scott stood guard at the window. Not wanting to awaken the officer, she continued down the hallway into the kitchen.

Will sipped coffee at the kitchen table. He must have sensed her presence because he looked up and cracked a natural smile. "Did you sleep okay?"

He automatically stood and greeted her with a hug.

"Sure, pretty good considering the circumstances."

"Bree left you some scones, and I made a fresh pot of coffee." He turned to grab a mug off the counter.

"I'll get it, thanks."

Her phone vibrated with a call and she answered. "Vaughn."

"It's SSA Bonner, returning your call."

"Good morning, sir." She straightened. "I thought you'd want an update—"

"You're supposed to be on vacation, not chasing a lead I specifically told you was off-limits."

"Sir, I—"

"Do you have any idea what you've done, Agent Vaughn? You've screwed up an eighteen-month investigation."

"I don't understand."

"Another team at the bureau had been working the David Price angle, trying to get enough leverage on him to make him roll on his partners."

"I had no idea."

"It was above your pay grade. And now Price is dead, and potentially so is your career."

"Wait, what?"

"It isn't always about you and your crusades, Agent Vaughn. I've told you that over and over again. We can't have agents who won't take orders. Therefore, you're suspended until further notice."

The room seemed to close in around her. She glanced at Will, his remarkable green eyes studying her with concern. She wanted to go to him again, be held in his strong, comforting arms. He believed in her. He believed she was an honorable crusader with an altruistic mission to protect people.

And that gave her strength.

"I disagree with this course of action," she said to her boss.

"You can appeal with personnel. But consider what your supervisors will say when asked about working with you, about how you've constantly challenged their authority. I'm not sure you were ever meant to be a part of our team, Agent Vaughn."

"Because I don't give up?" she said, her voice rising in pitch.

Bonner sighed heavily into the phone. "No, Sara." He hesitated. "Because of your tunnel vision. You only see what you're looking at, not anything else, or anyone else around you. If you'd been more aware of the people around you, you would have picked up on the cues that there was something else in the works regarding LHP. Other agents did, and they backed off, but you couldn't, because you shut out everything else."

"I thought focus made me a good agent."

"It does, to a point. You also have to trust your coworkers and the system, and that's where you disconnect. You don't trust anyone or anything besides your own instincts."

"Which were right in this case. Once I get my phone back, I'll have proof."

"I hope so, for your sake. If there's evidence on the phone and we're able to use it to build a case against LHP, my superiors might reconsider your suspension. Until then, you cannot act on the authority of our office, and I need to ask you to turn in your ID and firearm when you return."

It felt as if she'd been slugged in the gut. He was stripping away her identity.

"I…I'm not sure when I'm coming back," she said, her voice sounding foreign to her.

"Do what's necessary to help the local authorities in the Price homicide as a witness only, not as an agent." Bonner paused. "For what it's worth, I am sorry, and I wish you the best of luck. Goodbye, Sara."

She stared blindly at her phone.

"What is it?" Will touched her arm.

"I've been suspended."

"Oh, honey. I am so sorry."

"He accused me of only thinking about myself, of only seeing what I'm focused on, nothing else around me." She sighed. "He said I can't work with a team."

"Then, he doesn't know you very well."

"It sounds as if the only chance I have of keeping my job is the evidence on my phone."

"Come here." Will pulled her into an embrace.

She felt broken, betrayed, a complete failure. If only they would have told her about the other team investigating LHP she would have dropped it as ordered. But she hadn't because she'd thought they were giving up too easily.

A man cleared his throat, and Will released Sara. Nate hesitated in the doorway of the kitchen.

"She got some bad news," Will said.

"Unfortunately, I've got more bad news." Nate held up Sara's phone as he stepped into the kitchen. Scott also joined them.

"The video file is not retrievable," Nate said. "We can't use it to prove who killed David Price."

There went her job, plus LaRouche and Harrington would get away with murder and pin suspicion on Sara.

"That's unacceptable," she said.

Maybe Bonner thought her determination was a bad thing, yet in this case, it was her best defense.

"Didn't you say you knew a tech?" she asked Will.

"Yes, Zack Carter. He works here at the resort."

"I could get it to him," Scott offered.

"Let's try it, Nate," Will said. "I mean, what have we got to lose?"

"Even if Zack somehow gets the file, we couldn't use that in a court of law," Nate countered.

"LaRouche and Harrington wouldn't need to know that, at least not when you initially question them, right?" Sara offered.

Nate raised an eyebrow. "I suppose not."

"We could still use the recording to our advantage," she said.

The back door opened and Bree came inside with Fiona. "Oh, hey, everybody. Text alert went out. They're sending K9 teams to search for David Price's body on the east side of Granite Ridge."

"On the east side?" Will questioned.

"Yeah, why?"

"Because I found Sara on the west side of Echo Mountain. You have a map?"

"Sure." Bree went to her pack across the room and pulled a map out of a side pocket.

"What are you thinking?" Nate asked.

"That they're sending SAR teams to the wrong location."

Will spread the map out on the table and pointed to a small lake. "When this is where I found Sara."

"Sara, do you know where you camped the night you and David fell?" Nate questioned.

"We hiked up to Flatrock Overlook, then went west another two miles, so right about here." She pointed. "I fell down this side, and David was hurled off the trail toward the north."

"Which makes sense, because she ended up by the lake," Will said. "But Nate, look at how far away that campsite is from Granite Ridge."

"LaRouche and Harrington are sending search teams on a wild goose chase," Sara said.

"Because they don't want anyone finding the body," Nate offered.

"Which means there might be evidence on the body implicating LaRouche and Harrington," Sara said.

"Or they think David is still alive down there," Nate said.

They all shared a concerned look.

"It's happened before," Bree said. "A hiker has survived a nasty fall."

Nate's phone buzzed on his belt. He ripped it off, studied the message and looked at Sara. "It's my chief. LaRouche and Harrington are in town. They're demanding I lock you up."

FOURTEEN

Instead of locking Sara up, Nate scheduled a meeting with the chief and LaRouche and Harrington.

Then Nate made a call to the search and rescue command officer. "I have a witness who claims David Price fell off the north side of Echo Mountain."

Sara, Will, Bree and Scott anxiously listened in.

"I understand.…Uh-huh. Thanks." Nate ended the call with a frustrated groan. "They won't change their plan to search the east side of Granite Ridge."

"Then, they'll never find David Price," Sara protested.

"I'll talk to the chief. Maybe he's got more influence with SAR."

"What about LaRouche and Harrington's demands to lock me up?" Sara asked.

Nate looked at Sara, then Will. "I have no choice."

"Nate, think about this," Will argued.

"No, he's right," Sara said, putting her hand on Will's arm. "Bringing me in for questioning is proper procedure."

"Why do I feel like there's a 'but' at the end of that sentence?" Nate said, crossing his arms over his chest.

"But if you arrest me, and they find out I'm FBI, they'll bury any evidence of wrongdoing. If they cover their tracks, more people will die from the release of their drug, and if SAR searches the wrong area, David Price, our best chance at stopping them, will never be found, and what if he's alive?"

"That's a lot of ifs," Nate said.

Sara released a sigh. "I messed up by going after this on my own, I get it. Let me help you make it right."

"What do you think?" Nate asked Scott, a former cop.

"I guess it depends how badly you want to keep your job versus putting away the elitist jerks."

"You up for a search mission?" Nate asked Will.

"You bet."

"I'm coming," Sara said.

"No, it's not safe—"

"I can show you exactly where David fell," she interrupted Will.

"We need Sara on the team," Nate said. "Scott, you keep an eye on things back here."

"Fiona and I could help if we had something of David Price's so she could catch his scent," Bree offered.

"They have some items at the command center," Nate said. "We'll swing by, then head up into the mountains." Nate glanced at Scott. "If that's okay with you."

"Wait a minute, you're asking his permission to let me go on the mission?" Bree planted her hands on her hips and narrowed her eyes at Nate.

Scott went to her and brushed hair back away from her face in a sweet gesture. "He knows I lie awake nights worrying about you when you're on a mission, and this one has an added element of danger. I have total confidence in your abilities, love, but I don't trust these guys."

"Yeah, and LaRouche and Harrington might have their own guys searching the mountains, too," Sara said.

"Then, we'd better get going and find him first," Bree said with a lift of her chin.

Scott kissed her and looked at Nate. "You heard the woman. You guys better get going."

Three hours later, Sara, Will, Nate and Bree, along with her golden retriever, were closing in on the spot where David Price should have landed after being flung over the mountainside by Victor LaRouche. Sara had taped her ribs so they didn't hurt too much, and kept her wrist close to her stomach for added protection. Nothing was going to stop her from going on this mission— a dangerous mission that might cost Nate his job, and worse. An encounter with thugs out here in the wilderness could be disastrous.

Nate said they had today to work with, then it would be over. He'd have to officially question Sara about David's death, taking into account LaRouche and Harrington's false accusations.

And the chances of finding David Price in one day? Well, she didn't want to think about that. She needed to stay focused.

"Your boss is wrong," Will suddenly said.

Sara eyed him. "Excuse me?"

"You're working with a team right now." He winked.

Warmth filled her chest at the sight of his smile, the teasing wink and the adorable knit hat he wore that made him look young and untouched by the grief she knew he'd survived.

"Stop flirting," Nate said over his shoulder.

"That obvious, huh?" Will answered.

"Nah," Nate said sarcastically.

"Wait, she's got something," Bree said as they approached a thick mass of brush. "Okay, girl, go find him."

Bree released her and the dog took off. The four of them followed.

Will hung back, probably to make sure Sara was okay. As she eyed Nate and Bree in front of them, and Will beside her, she realized the truth to his words: she was part of a team. She liked the feeling.

"I see something!" Bree called.

Nate put out his hand, indicating he'd go first to investigate. The dog barked excitedly and Bree commanded her to heel.

Sara, Will and Bree approached Nate, who stood beside a small cave.

"You think he's in there?" Will asked.

"One way to find out." Nate clicked on his flashlight and headed into the cave. Sara and Will followed, and Bree waited beside the entrance with Fiona.

Heart pounding, Sara hoped, she prayed, that David was still alive. A part of her felt guilty for not being able to stop Vic LaRouche from throwing him off the cliff.

"David? David Price, this is the police," Nate called. "We're here to help."

Nate hesitated and turned to Will and Sara. "That's far enough for you two. Wait here." Nate continued into the cave while Sara and Will waited anxiously for news about David's condition.

Will interlaced his fingers with Sara's. They waited, the passing seconds feeling like hours.

"Get away from me!" a man shouted.

"No, wait—" They heard a grunt and a thud.

Then silence.

"Out, now." Will pushed Sara toward the exit.

She got safely outside and Bree peered around Sara. "Where's Will?"

Sara spun around. "I thought he was right behind me. He must still be in there." Sara instinctively started back inside. Bree grabbed her arm.

"Wait." Bree dug in her pack and pulled out a small black canister. "To defend yourself."

"Pepper spray?"

"Long story."

Sara turned back to the cave.

"We got him!" Will called out.

A minute later, Will and Nate exited the cave, propping up a disoriented David Price.

"He's okay?" Sara said, shocked.

"Dehydrated and out of it," Nate said, rubbing his forehead where a gash dripped blood. "Bree can you get me some gauze or something? And get David some water."

"Sure."

"He hit you?" Sara asked.

"Probably thought I was a bear."

She studied Will.

"I'm fine," he said. "Talked him down so we could bring him out."

They led David out of the cave to a small clearing and sat him on a boulder. "David Price, I'm Detective Walsh of the Echo Mountain PD. Can you tell us what happened?"

Sara remained silent, not wanting to influence David's recollection.

"They came at me." He looked at Nate with wide eyes. "Huge bees!"

Will offered the guy some water and he drank.

"Do you remember how you ended up down here?" Nate asked as he pressed gauze against his own head wound.

"Do you remember going on a mountain excursion?" Sara said, then eyed Nate, hoping she hadn't crossed a line. He was still focused on David.

"You went on a hiking trip with your partners," Nate offered.

"No!" David stood abruptly and swung his arms. Will got behind him and put him in a hold that rendered him immobile.

"Calm down, sir," Nate said. "We're your search and rescue team, remember?"

"Search and rescue," David repeated, and stopped struggling. "Oh, yeah, sorry."

Will released him and David sat on the boulder again.

"Nice hold," Sara said to Will.

He winked. "Gotta be ready for when the girls bring their boyfriends home."

It amazed her that Will could find humor while embroiled in this intense situation.

"Tell us what you remember about your fall," Nate asked David.

"He threw me... My business partner threw me over the edge." He looked at Sara and scrunched his eyebrows. "I know you, don't I?"

"I was on the trail guide team that led you into the mountains."

David nodded, his gaze drifting to his hands.

"She helped us find you, Mr. Price," Nate offered.

David nodded at Sara. "Thank you. I wouldn't have survived another night."

"Can you walk?" Nate asked.

"I think so."

"If not, we've got a litter," Nate offered.

"No, no, I can walk."

"Did you injure yourself in the fall?" Will asked.

"My arm. I may have broken my arm."

Will examined David's arm. "We can splint it temporarily. Should we call for another team to help bring him back?"

"I'd rather do this on our own for now," Nate said.

David suddenly slumped over. Will eased him down to lie the ground.

"You okay to help me carry him down?" Will asked Nate.

"Yeah, I'm fine." Nate rubbed his head.

"Not so fine if you've got a concussion," Will countered. "Call for another team. There aren't enough of us to carry you down if you pass out."

Nate nodded. "I'll call for backup."

"LaRouche and Harrington will find out where we are," Sara said.

"Unofficial backup," Nate explained. "Friends of mine." He yanked his radio off his belt and squinted to see it.

"Blurred vision?" Will asked.

"Take care of David," Nate ordered.

Will and Sara shared a frustrated look as Will continued splinting David's arm.

"It's Nate," he said into his phone. "We found him where I marked it on the map. He's wounded and we need help carrying him down. Yep.…What?…Okay, will do." He looked back at the group. "They'll be here as soon as possible."

David moaned and opened his eyes, blinking as he focused on the towering trees. "I'm still here. I can't be here." He struggled to sit up.

"Hang on, buddy," Will said.

"I have to get back to my family. It's Christmas," he said.

"You've got time. Christmas is two weeks away," Bree offered.

"If you're up to it we can start down," Nate said. "Help is on its way. Chances are we'll run into them and they can carry you the rest of the way."

"I can do it. I can walk," David said.

Will and Nate helped David stand up, and they stayed close, probably worried he'd collapse again. As they hiked down, Bree tried making conversation with Sara, but Sara was more focused on her surroundings. The slightest sound could indicate a potential threat. They were far from safe, and wouldn't be until David had given his official statement.

My business partner threw me over the edge.

Mitigated relief drifted across Sara's shoulders as she considered the significance of David's declaration. It was the proof she needed to clear her name and put an end to LaRouche and Harrington's sinister plan.

And maybe, just maybe, she'd be able to keep her job.

An hour later, a prickling sensation tickled the back of Sara's neck. She'd learned to never question that instinct.

"Everybody down," she ordered, and shoved Will and David down on the ground behind a fallen tree trunk.

A gunshot rang out across the mountain range.

"No!" David cried.

Bree stood there, motionless, the dog barking by her side. Sara dived at Bree, yanking her behind a boulder.

"Tell Fiona to be quiet," Sara said, not wanting the innocent dog to become a target.

Bree looked at Sara with a confused, terrified expression.

"Bree, you're okay," Sara said, squeezing her arm. "Tell the dog to be quiet."

"Fiona, no bark," Bree said.

Fiona nudged Sara's hand so she'd release her grip on Bree. "She's fine, Fiona," Sara said. "Bree, tell her you're fine."

"Good girl," Bree said. "Mama's okay. Right here, honey." The dog settled down beside Bree, who still looked shell-shocked.

"Will, are you okay?" Bree called out.

"David and I are good."

"Nate?" Sara said.

Silence.

"Detective Walsh!" she called out with more force. "Nate!"

Nothing. Sara peered around the boulder and saw Nate's blue jacket. He was down. She took a step to go to him…

Another shot rang out. She darted behind the boulder.

"Sara!" Will shouted.

"I'm fine."

Sara wasn't anxious or panicked. Instead, she suddenly grew calm. She had to protect this group of people who a week ago were strangers, and today meant much more.

Especially Will.

"Everyone stay where you are." Sara turned to Bree. "You're safe back here. Keep Fiona close and quiet, okay?"

Bree nodded.

Sara darted between trees and bushes to get closer to Nate. He lay facedown on the trail. Exposed. "Nate?"

He groaned. "Yeah."

"You need to move. Stay low," she coached from the bushes.

He shifted onto hands and knees, rather one hand, because his other hand clutched his shoulder.

"Come on," she urged.

Nate crouch-ran across the trail to Sara.

A third shot rang out.

Nate ducked, kept running and collapsed beside Sara. He winced as he gripped his shoulder. "Unbelievable."

"How bad?"

"I think through and through."

She pulled a scarf from around her neck. "Move your hand so I can put pressure against the wound."

"Don't worry about me. Take care of the others."

Sara ignored him, pried his hand away from the wound and shoved the scarf in place.

"You have to protect..." Nate's voice trailed off and his head lolled to the side.

Between his head injury and the bullet wound, he was out of it.

"Bree?" she called.

"Yes?"

"I need you to come over here and help Nate."

"Won't they shoot at me?"

"You've got good cover if you stay behind trees and bushes. And stay low."

Bree and Fiona darted to where Sara was tending to Nate. No shots were fired, which confirmed Sara's suspicion that the shooter didn't want to kill all of them, probably just David and Sara.

"Keep pressure on the wound," Sara directed Bree.

"Okay."

Sara grabbed Nate's radio and called in. "Base, this is Sara Vaughn. We have an officer down and we're taking fire. We need backup. Our location is—" She paused. "Will, best guess where we are?"

"About one and a half kilometers north of the resort on Cedar Grove Trail."

She repeated the information into the radio. There was no response.

"Base, do you read me, over?" she said.

When no one responded, she decided to take action.

"Bree, stay with Nate." Sara grabbed Nate's gun and went to check on Will, again staying low. As she scrambled across the damp terrain, a shot cracked through the air.

She dived over the fallen tree trunk and landed beside Will and David. "How's it going over here?"

Will narrowed his eyes. "Just peachy."

"David?" she said, sitting up.

A blank expression creased his features. "We're all going to die."

"Nope, not today."

"What's the plan?" Will asked.

"I'll draw his fire, then you're going to have to use this." She handed Will the gun.

He looked at it. "I don't do guns, and I'm not letting you run out there like a duck at a shooting gallery."

"It's our best option."

"There's got to be another one."

"I'm open for ideas." She placed the gun beside Will and turned to ready herself for the hundred-yard sprint. She wasn't even sure where she was going, yet she had to draw the guy out of hiding.

She felt a hand on her shoulder and she turned to look into Will's warm green eyes.

"Be careful," he said. And he brushed a kiss against her lips.

It was all so surreal: the smell of fresh pine, the kiss and the incredible warmth from his lips that drifted across her shoulders. How could something so beautiful be happening at the same time as something so ugly?

Ugly? She'd never thought of her work as ugly before.

Will broke the kiss. "Try calling for backup again, please?"

She looked beyond him at David, who stared straight ahead at nothing in particular. He looked to be in shock.

She tried the radio again. "Base, we have an officer down, over."

Sara and Will held each other's gazes.

"Base, come in, over." Another few seconds passed. "They can't hear us."

With a sigh, Will closed his eyes. She guessed he was praying. A few seconds later he leaned forward and kissed her cheek, as if to say goodbye.

As if he feared she would be shot and killed.

"Do what you think is best," he said, his voice hoarse.

She hesitated, realizing how deeply he cared about her, and she him.

"This is Chief Washburn. We're sending a team, over."

Sara snapped her gaze from Will's and eyed the radio in shock. "Thanks, Chief," she said. "Nate called for a SAR team to carry down David Price. I'm worried about them being in harm's way, over."

"There are two police officers on that team. We estimate they're only ten minutes out from your location. How bad is Nate hit, over?"

"Shoulder wound. He also suffered a head injury and is currently unconscious, over."

"Doc Spencer is with that first team, plus we have another team of cops headed your way. Stay put and stay safe, over."

"You got it, over."

Another shot rang out. Bree shrieked in fear.

"This is ridiculous." Sara grabbed the gun, ready to go out there and shoot blindly at their tormentor.

Will placed his hand over hers. She hesitated and looked into his eyes.

"Help is on the way," he said. "There's no need for you to put yourself at risk."

"I can't sit here and do nothing while they terrorize us. I refuse to hide anymore." She peered around the tree trunk.

"Sara?" Will said.

Irritated, she turned to him.

"Staying here is not the dishonorable thing to do," he said. "His goal is to draw you out. If you go after him, he wins. He will have taken away the only person in our group with the skills to defend us. We need you, Sara." He hesitated. "I need you."

His emerald eyes, so sincere and compassionate, pinned her in place. She couldn't move if she tried.

"Okay?" he said. "Will you stay and protect us?"

"I… Sure."

He motioned for her to sit beside him.

"No, I'll keep watch, in case he advances on us," she said.

Another shot rang out.

"Really?" she snapped.

Fiona burst into a frantic round of barks.

"What's he shooting at? He can't see us," Will said.

"It's called intimidation," Sara said. "Bree, it's okay, he can't see you. You're safe!"

"I don't feel very safe," she called back.

"I hate this," Sara muttered.

"Then, let's change it," Will offered.

"What are you talking about?"

"If there's one thing I've learned in my thirty-four years, it's that in any given situation we have a choice," Will said. "A choice to be fearful or to feel loved."

"Uh…I know you're religious and all that, but even Jesus wouldn't feel loved if someone was shooting at him."

He cracked a smile. "Probably not. Since we're stuck here until help arrives, and this man's goal is to paralyze us with fear, let's make the choice to feel something else."

And then, Will started singing.

"Joy to the world, the Lord is come!" his deep voice rang out.

Sara felt her jaw drop as she stared at this man with the peaceful demeanor and beautiful voice, and wondered how she'd ended up here, in the company of such an amazing human being. They were being used as target practice, yet he sang instead of panicking.

Then Bree's voice chimed in, and even David croaked out a few words here and there.

Sara shook her head with wonder. She could only guess what their assailant was thinking—probably that they were all crazy.

"Repeat the sounding joy," Will sang, encouraging her to sing along.

She did, but kept her focus glued to the rugged terrain where the shooter hid, waiting for an opportunity to take one of them out.

"Repeat the sounding joy," she sang softly, her eyes scanning the area.

"This is Officer McBride. We hear you, over," his voice said through the radio.

"Officer McBride, this is Sara Vaughn. Nate's been shot and is unconscious. The shooter is still out there, over."

"Ten-four."

"Who's with you?" she asked.

"Officer Duggins, Doc Spencer and Scott Becket."

She withdrew behind the tree trunk and spoke in a low voice. "We need to flush this guy out of hiding, over."

"We're on it. Keep singing to distract him, over."

She nodded at Will. "You heard them. They want us to keep singing."

Will started "Joy to the World" from the beginning, and the group chimed in. Adjusting her fingers on the gun grip, she aimed around the tree trunk in case the shooter planned one final suicide move to kill David Price.

"Police, put your weapon down!" a voice shouted.

Three shots rang out.

She hoped they didn't kill the attacker, because he could provide more evidence against LaRouche and Harrington if he rolled on them.

She spotted movement behind Bree and Nate.

Sara aimed Nate's weapon…

Scott darted up and over shrubbery and landed beside Bree. He held her in his arms. Sara eased her finger off the trigger.

"Breathe," Will said.

She took a slow breath in.

"I've got to get out of here!" David shouted.

Out of the corner of her eye, Sara spotted David take off.

"No!" Will went after him.

"Will!" Sara shouted.

A shot rang out.

Sara sprung out of their hiding spot.

All she could think was *Will was shot!*

The shooter was heading her way. Totally focused on Will and David, both on the ground.

She aimed her weapon. "Hey!"

The guy turned.

Gotta keep him alive.

She fired, hitting him in the shoulder. He kept coming. She fired again, hitting him in the thigh.

He went down and kept crawling toward David and Will.

She sprinted to the shooter and stepped on his firing hand. Officer McBride and his team raced up to Sara.

Oh, God, Will can't die. You can't let him die.

"Doctor Spencer," Sara said. "Will and David… I think one of them was shot…" She could hear herself stumbling, not making much sense.

"What about Detective Walsh?" Officer McBride asked.

"Over here!" Scott called out.

"Spike, go help Nate." Officer McBride stepped closer to Sara. She couldn't take her eyes off the shooter, or her hand still aiming the gun at his back.

"Agent Vaughn?"

Sara glanced at Officer McBride.

With a nod of respect, he said, "Well-placed shots."

She nodded her thanks. "Was he the only one?"

"Yes, ma'am. We searched the immediate area. It's clear. Do you recognize him?"

"No," Sara said.

The shooter attempted to crawl away.

"Yeah?" Officer McBride dropped and kneeled on his back. He pulled his arms behind his back to cuff him. "Where do you think you're going?"

Sara blinked, seeing the gun still at the end of her extended arm. She was okay. They got the shooter.

But Will… Was he…? She lowered her arm and closed her eyes.

"Sara?"

She opened her eyes to Will's tentative smile. They went into each other's arms.

"Was David Price shot?" Officer McBride asked.

"No. He's suffering from dehydration, a possible concussion and a broken arm," Will said.

"Well put, Doctor Rankin," Dr. Spencer said as he examined David.

"Command, this is Officer McBride," he spoke into his radio. "We've located the injured parties, over." He clicked off the radio. "Scott, how's Nate?"

"I'm fine," Nate called back.

"He needs a litter," Scott countered.

"What are you, my mother?" Nate said.

"And he's belligerent from the head injury," Bree said.

"This is Chief Washburn. Have the assailants been neutralized, over?"

"Yes sir, just one, over," Officer McBride answered.

"Is Will Rankin okay, over?" the chief asked through the radio.

Everyone looked at Will.

"I'm fine," Will said.

"He's fine, over," Officer McBride said.

"A SAR team is on the way to assist. Send Will Rankin down ASAP."

"What, why?" Will said.

"Chief, is there a problem?" Officer McBride prompted.

"His mother-in-law is missing."

FIFTEEN

Will paled. "My girls," he muttered, and headed down the trail.

Sara glanced at Nate for permission to follow Will. After all, she'd shot a man with Nate's gun, and perhaps he wanted her to stay at the scene.

"Go," Nate said.

She took off after Will, but didn't crowd him. She didn't want him to feel smothered.

More like, she didn't want to see his face twisted with panic and emotional turmoil. She wasn't sure she could handle that.

Coward, she scolded herself. He'd spent the past few hours keeping everyone sane and calm, and she didn't have the guts to do the same for him?

If she offered comfort and he pushed her away, she'd ignore the rejection and keep on trying.

"Will," she said, close enough to touch him.

He shook his head. "I can't believe I've put her in danger."

"Hey, hey, let's not assume anything here." She finally touched his arm.

He acted as if he didn't even feel her. She let her hand fall to her side.

"Even if it is related to the case, this is not your fault. You did not willingly put your family in danger. LaRouche and Harrington are the ones who deserve the blame."

She thought he might have nodded. She'd never seen him like this, so lost and closed off.

"I'm not sure..." His voice trailed off. "I'm not sure how I could live without them."

She darted in front of him and placed her hand against his chest. "Don't talk like that. There's no reason to hurt the girls, even if they have them, which I highly doubt."

He stepped around her. "Didn't know you had an optimistic streak, Agent Vaughn."

"Yeah, I'm full of surprises. Now stop going to those dark places and show me how to pray."

He snapped his attention to her. "What?"

"You heard me. So do I need to fold my hands together or do anything special? Look up to heaven or what?"

"You don't have to do this," he said.

"I want to."

His frown eased a bit. "We could recite the Lord's Prayer, I suppose."

As they made their way back to the resort, they repeated the Lord's Prayer, the words feeling unusually natural as they rolled off her tongue. Color had come back to Will's cheeks, and he had stopped clenching his jaw every few minutes.

For the first time in her life, Sara felt a connection to God as she helped Will avoid the pitfalls of fear and focus on the guiding light of hope.

Mary's heart raced, pounding against her chest like a jackhammer. Where was she? She slowly blinked her eyes open. White surrounded her. Was she dead?

I'm coming, Megan, I'm coming.

No, Mary couldn't die. Who would take care of the girls? Will was always off on his dangerous adventures, putting his own needs first, before the girls'. And while Edward was a fun grandpa, he wasn't a disciplinarian. Without Mary's influence in their lives, the girls would grow up wild and lost.

She fingered a trail of warm blood trickling down her forehead. No, she wasn't dead. Yet.

She pushed at the billowy white material—the airbag that

had saved her life. That was right, she had gone out to get construction paper for Marissa's art project, a project that her father should have helped her finish. But he was too busy saving some strange woman's life—a woman who brought trouble to Echo Mountain. Because of Sara, Mary and Ed were taking the girls out of town tomorrow for a few days.

On the way home from getting construction paper, Mary's tires had lost their grip on the slick road, and she had skidded over an embankment.

She looked left, then right. Surrounded by greenery, trees and bushes, she started to panic.

Then heavy white snow started to fall.

She unbuckled herself and looked over her shoulder. She'd landed at the bottom of a ravine.

In a few hours the car would be covered with snow and no one would even know she was down here. She pushed on the door. It wouldn't budge. She reached across the seat to the other side.

Shoved open the door.

It would only open so far. Not far enough to get her body out. Even if she did, how would she climb up to the street level without help?

Her phone—she had to call for help. Then she remembered leaving it behind because she didn't think she'd be gone that long.

"Somebody help! Help me!" she wailed.

She slammed her blood-smudged palm against the horn three times. Waited. Punched three more times.

She couldn't die this way, withering away, probably starving to death.

Alone.

Mama, I love you, but you're going to die a lonely old woman if you don't start softening your edges with the girls, Megan had lectured.

Mary couldn't help herself. She worried about everything and everyone, especially the girls, since their father seemed to let them do whatever they wanted. That was no way to raise a family.

Yet they adored him. Mary saw it in their eyes every time Claire and Marissa saw their dad after being apart for even a few hours.

Suddenly Mary wondered if all this anger she felt toward Will was really coming from somewhere other than worry. No, she was dizzy from the accident, that was all.

Be honest with yourself, Mary.

She finally admitted that her resentment and anger were born of fear, fear that the girls would forget their mother, Mary's pride and joy. Mary feared Will would bring another woman into their lives, they'd forget about their mom and Grandma would be cast aside like a used paper towel.

"No!" she shouted, gasping for breath as fear smothered her.

She slammed her palms on the horn again, desperate to stay alive, to see her granddaughters, to hold them, to show them she did, in fact, have softer edges.

"I can't die!" she cried, slamming her hands on the horn.

Something thudded against the passenger door. She shrieked.

Will shot her a smile and a casual wave. "Looks as if you took a wrong turn, Nanny."

"Oh, Will!" she sobbed with relief.

Another man came up beside Will, about Will's age with a full beard and jet-black hair. Mary didn't recognize him.

"Is she okay?" the bearded fellow asked.

"She'll be better when we get this door open."

They managed to get the door open. Will reached in and touched her shoulder.

Which only made her cry more.

"Hey, it's okay, Mary," Will said in a gentle voice.

She couldn't stop crying. With relief, with gratitude and maybe even with shame.

Will, of all people, had found her. He'd saved her. She'd been so nasty to him since Megan's death, so judgmental.

"We've located her," Will said into a radio. "She seems okay, a little banged up." He hesitated. "Mary, where are you hurt?"

"Everywhere." She sighed.

"Can you be a little more specific?"

"My head's bleeding and my chest aches. That's about it."

"That's plenty." Will clicked on his radio. "We need a litter and two more guys." He nodded at Mary. "You're going to be fine."

"I can't believe you found me."

"Of course I found you. My girls would be lost without their Nanny. Griff here has got more medical training than me, so we're going to switch spots, okay?"

She squeezed his hand, not wanting to let go. "Could you… Would you be able to… Never mind." She didn't have the gall to ask him to stay close considering the way she'd treated him.

She released Will's hand and he backed out. His partner climbed into the car. "Hi, Mary, I'm Griffin Keane. I'm going to examine your head wound to see how serious it is, okay?"

"Sure." As he reached out to remove hair from the wound, she closed her eyes.

A moment later, she felt Will's hand settle on her shoulder from behind. He'd climbed into the backseat.

She reached up and placed her hand over his. "I get it now," she said. "This is what you do with your time off, rescue little old ladies."

"Little, big, old, young, we don't discriminate," Will said. "We make sure we're ready to go when and where we're needed."

"On call for others," Griffin muttered as he placed a bandage on Mary's forehead.

As understanding opened her heart to compassion, Mary

felt more alive than she ever had. She looked over her shoulder at Will. “I’m so sorry.”

“Aw, don’t worry about it. Ed never liked this car anyway.”

“That’s not what I meant.”

He winked. “I know.”

Two hours later, Will waited at the hospital for news about Mary. He had truly felt God’s presence when he’d rescued her from the car. It was the first time he’d felt a connection to Mary: a positive, healthy connection.

As they had waited for the second team to assist, Mary had confessed her fears about Will and the girls forgetting Megan. He’d assured her that would *never* happen because he and Mary would remind the girls what a wonderful mother Megan had been.

Will closed his eyes and sighed. Through all the danger and threat of violence over the past few days, he’d come to accept that Megan hadn’t pushed Will away because she hadn’t had confidence in him as a husband to take care of her. Rather, she had feared for him as a father, a challenging position for even the strongest person. Megan had wanted Will to practice being a single parent while she was still around to advise.

So much sacrifice. So much love.

“How about some tea?”

He opened his eyes to Sara, the determined federal agent he’d somehow fallen in love with.

“Sure,” he said, and she handed him the paper cup. He clenched his jaw against the awareness that sparked between them every time they touched.

She sat down next to him. “What aren’t you telling me?”

“Excuse me?” He snapped his attention to her.

“That jaw-clench thing usually means trouble.”

“No, Mary’s good, pretty minor injuries considering.

When I first saw the car at the bottom of that ravine…" His voice trailed off.

Sara touched his arm. "But she's okay."

"She is, and I think narrowly escaping death has changed her a bit."

"It usually does." Sara studied her teacup. "Not always for the better."

He guessed she was referring to her father's death.

"Daddy! Daddy!" Claire and Marissa sprinted across the hospital lobby. He put the teacup on the table beside him and opened his arms. They launched themselves at him and he held them close.

"How are my girls?"

"Hey, Will. Thank-you doesn't seem like enough," his father-in-law said.

"I should be thanking you for taking care of my rascals."

Marissa leaned back. "Daddy, I'm not a rascal. Did you really rescue Nanny from a car wreck?"

"I did."

"Does she have a broken nose?" Marissa asked.

"No, what makes you ask that?" Will realized Claire's face was still buried against his shoulder.

"Because Olivia's mother got in a car wreck and her nose was broken, and she wore this big white bandage here." She pressed little-girl fingers on her nose.

"Well, Nanny's nose is fine. She's got some scratches and bruises. She'll be A-OK."

"Hi, Miss Sara." Marissa went in for a hug and Sara hugged back.

Will turned his attention to Claire. "Baby doll?"

She tipped her head and whispered into his ear. "I know about the guy in the mountains trying to shoot you. I didn't tell Marissa. She'd have nightmares."

His heart sank. He didn't want either of his daughters knowing about the danger. "I'm okay, sweetie," he whispered back. "Miss Sara protected us."

"Mr. Varney," a nurse called from the ER doorway. "Your wife can see you now."

"I'm going, I'm going!" Marissa rushed to her grandfather's side.

"What about you, Claire bear?" Ed asked.

"I need to stay with Daddy," her muffled voice said against his neck.

Ed took Marissa into the examining area.

"I should give you some privacy," Sara said.

"No, wait." Will reached out and grabbed her hand. "Don't leave."

Sara nodded and clung to Will's hand.

Claire sniffled against his neck. She was crying.

Compassion colored Sara's blue eyes as she studied his little girl. She'd make such a great mother some day, a fierce protector. He suspected she would brush off such a suggestion.

She slipped her hand from his and reached out to stroke the back of Claire's head. "Your daddy was so brave. He was never frightened, and he made us all feel safe."

Claire turned her head to look at Sara. "He did?"

"I did?" Will said.

"Yep, and you know how?"

Claire shook her head that she didn't.

"He sang."

"He's a good singer."

When Sara looked at Will, his heart warmed in his chest.

"He's good at many things," Sara said softly.

He sensed someone approach from the left. "Will, where is he? Where's Nate?"

Cassie McBride towered over him.

"He's being patched up in the ER," Will said.

"I'm fine, thank you very much," Bree said, walking up to them.

"Bree, Bree, you're here, too!" Cassie threw her arms around her sister and hugged her tight.

"Yeah, I thought you heard about—"

"Where's Nate?" Cassie broke the hold and looked into her sister's eyes.

"In there." She pointed.

Cassie dashed toward the examining area as Nate was being wheeled out.

"Are you okay?" Cassie said. "Where were you shot? Does it hurt? Where are they taking you?"

"Yes… The shoulder… No, thanks to the pain meds, and I don't know." Nate tipped his head toward the orderly. "Where are you taking me? To Hawaii, I hope."

Cassie narrowed her eyes at Nate. "How much pain medication?"

"I dunno, enough?"

With Claire in his arms, Will walked over to Nate, and Sara followed.

Nate extended his hand and they shook. "Hey, buddy. Hey, Claire. Your daddy's a hero, did you know that?"

Claire nodded. "Miss Sara told me."

Nate nodded at Sara. "You talk to the chief?"

"Not yet. He's taking David's statement."

"I need to get him upstairs so he can rest," the orderly said.

"I'm coming with," Cassie said, tagging alongside the stretcher.

"He said rest, Cassie, not answer twenty-seven questions," Nate said.

"I've never asked that many."

"I'll tell ya what, I'll start counting."

"Why are you being such a wise guy? Do you have a concussion? Have they done an MRI? How'd you get that cut on your forehead?" Her voice softened as they turned the corner.

"She talks too much," Claire said.

"She only talks like that when she's nervous," Will said.

"Why's she nervous?" Claire asked.

"Because she was so worried about Detective Nate."

"Ooh," Claire said. "I get it." She giggled.

"Yeah? What do you get, huh?" Will tickled her tummy as the three of them wandered back to the lounge.

"Sara Vaughn?" Chief Washburn said coming down the hall.

"You ready for my statement?" she asked.

"Yes. I need you to come to the station with me."

Two men turned the corner behind the chief. From Sara's tense reaction, Will assumed they were LaRouche and Harrington.

"Can't she give it to you here, chief?" Will said.

Chief Washburn approached Sara and Will. "I'm afraid not. David Price has given his statement. He claims Sara shoved him off the trail."

SIXTEEN

Will stood there in shock, devastated by the false accusation. A few hours ago David Price had admitted that Mr. LaRouche shoved him off the mountain, and now he was blaming Sara?

The only thing keeping Will from blowing a gasket was the fact he held Claire in his arms.

Sara touched his shoulder, and Will ripped his attention from LaRouche and Harrington's victorious smirks.

With a resigned expression she said, "It's okay. I'll figure things out from here. Take care of your family." She reached out and brushed her thumb across Claire's cheek. "It was nice seeing you again, sweetie."

"You, too, Miss Sara."

With a sad smile, Sara turned and the chief handcuffed her. Will walked away so that wouldn't be the last image Claire would see of Sara: being led away in cuffs by the chief of police.

Will sensed LaRouche's and Harrington's arrogance, their satisfaction. Somehow they'd convinced David to change his story and accuse Sara of attempted murder. But how?

His father-in-law came out of the examining area with Marissa in tow.

"How's Mary?" Will asked.

"She'll be fine once they get her to a room. She was a little cranky and didn't want the girls seeing her like that—" he squeezed Marissa's hand "—so she asked us to wait out here."

"Would you mind watching the girls for a few minutes? I need to talk to Nate."

"Sure, sure."

Will put Claire down. "Stay close to your sister. I'll be right back."

"Okay, Daddy."

He hugged both his girls and went to see Nate. When he got into the elevator, he wondered if Nate was the right guy to be talking to right now. Will changed his mind and made his way to David Price's room.

Will was unsure what he'd say or how he'd persuade the man to admit the truth. Even if he could, David had given his official statement to the chief about Sara.

As he stepped into David's room, he heard a woman's voice behind the privacy curtain. Will hesitated.

"Send them away? Why would I send them away, David? They were so worried about you when you didn't come home. We all were."

"Listen to me, Beth. It's best for everyone if they spend a little time with their cousins over break. I'm also going to hire security to be with them 24/7."

"Security? Why?"

"Our business is dangerous. I know that now."

"That woman's going to jail. She can't hurt you anymore."

"It's not her I'm worried about," he croaked. "It's my criminal partners."

"David," she said, shocked. "What are you talking about?"

"Abreivtas is dangerous. They knew it and pushed it through anyway. I found out and confronted them. That's when LaRouche shoved me over the cliff."

Will ripped the curtain back. "Then, why are you sending an innocent woman to jail?"

"Who are you and what are you doing here?" David's wife said. "I'm calling security." She reached for the phone.

David grabbed her wrist. "Don't."

She released the phone and waited.

"I owe this man my life," David said, nodding his thanks to Will.

"Then, tell the truth," Will countered.

David sighed. "I can't." He squeezed his wife's hand and shook his head.

"David?" she said.

"I can't risk you having a car accident on the way to Pete's soccer practice, or Julianna's skating lessons or…or someone breaking into the house when I'm out of town," he croaked.

His wife's face paled with shock.

David narrowed his eyes at Will. "Do you have a family, Mr. Rankin?"

"Two girls."

"What would you do if someone threatened them?"

Will remembered the visceral panic that had coursed through him when he'd heard Mary had disappeared and he'd feared the girls were with her.

Will had feared the girls had been taken because of his involvement with Sara.

"Mr. Rankin?" David pushed.

"I'd do whatever was necessary to protect them."

"Then, don't judge me for trying to protect my family."

With a nod, Will left the couple alone. What now? Find Nate? Tell the chief what was going on? Who would believe Will, the man who'd fallen in love with a rogue FBI agent accused of attempted murder?

Will would contact Royce, one of the best attorneys in the county, to make sure she didn't go to jail for a crime she didn't commit. Perhaps Royce could leak damaging information to the proper authorities about Abreivtas.

"Don't get ahead of yourself," he said.

He'd get the girls settled at home and make his calls. Will did whatever was necessary to protect the people he loved, and Sara was now on that list.

Sara flung her arm over her eyes as she stretched out on a cot in Echo Mountain PD lockup.

She hadn't seen Will since the hospital last night. She

wondered if he'd given up on her, not that she'd blame him. Anyone involved with Sara would be sucked into a melee of problems, staring with her own traumatic childhood, and violent career. Make that her former career.

She'd failed. Miserably.

It didn't surprise her that David Price had changed his story. LaRouche and Harrington had obviously gotten to him, probably threatening David's kids and lovely wife.

Still, Sara hadn't thought she'd end up being arrested and going to jail. Being an FBI agent had to carry some weight with a jury, and once Nate testified that David had, in fact, claimed LaRouche threw him over the mountainside, well, that should be enough for reasonable doubt.

Unless LaRouche and Harrington were able to buy off the jury. No, she couldn't go there, nor did she want to give up on preventing Abreivtas from being distributed. How was she going to do that from a jail cell?

She had to stop her mind from spinning, and rely on others for help. Nate had stopped by earlier and praised her for how she'd handled herself in the mountains. He'd said he was determined to clear her name, as was Will, although Nate had asked Will to keep his distance from Sara. She agreed with that decision, of course, but missed him all the same.

The door to the cell area creaked open.

"Hello, Sara," Vic LaRouche said.

She sat up and glared at him. Ted Harrington stood right beside him. "You've won," Sara said. "Leave me alone."

"Not quite," LaRouche said. "Proving your innocence can be problematic for us. And we know you don't like problems."

"Neither do you, apparently. What did you do to David, threaten his kids or what?"

"We don't threaten. Threats are a bullying tactic, and infer you never mean to follow through." LaRouche leaned into the bars. "We leverage."

"Don't waste your time on me. I'm not fighting the charges."

"No, but your boyfriend is."

She sighed. "Don't have a boyfriend."

"Will Rankin."

She forced a disinterested look on her face. Psychopaths like LaRouche saw right through it.

"He's already contacted a top defense attorney. We can't have that kind of publicity, can we, Ted?"

"Wouldn't be good for business," Ted Harrington agreed.

"Right, the business of killing people," she snapped.

"We don't kill anyone. We offer approved medications to help people cope with the stresses of life," LaRouche said.

"Whatever. I'm going to jail. What more do you want from me?" she said.

With a maniacal smile, he slipped a photograph through the bars. It dropped to the floor. She glanced down at the smiling faces of Will, Claire and Marissa.

"Since you've been unable to convince Mr. Rankin to distance himself from all this, you leave us no choice. It will be a shame to orphan those adorable girls."

She charged the bars to grab him, but he leaned back, out of reach. "Leave that family alone!"

"Tell you what, we'll do just that on one condition."

She waited, clenching her jaw, wondering how much of this she had to endure.

"You'll take our lovely medication and go to sleep with the comfort of knowing the Rankin family will be safe, and the girls will grow up to live long and happy lives."

She eyed the pill in his hand. Now what? If she didn't take it, they'd probably send another assassin, this time to kill Will. The thought of a world without Will's smiling face and warmhearted laugh was not a world worth living in.

She had no choice. She'd take the pill, and bury it in the side of her mouth.

This was going to be a tough sell, yet she had to do it. If she took the pill and something went wrong…

It would be her last sacrifice.

To save Will and the girls.

"Fine." She motioned with her fingers.

"Oh, no, lovely. Open your mouth."

She hesitated. There was no going back now.

"Or were you going to trick us?" LaRouche raised an eyebrow.

She cracked her mouth open. He reached into the cell and grabbed her hair. With a yank, he tossed the pill down her throat and slammed her jaw shut. Her eyes watered. She had no choice but to swallow.

And she did.

He released her with a jerk and she stumbled back. Her gaze drifted to the photo on the floor. She kneeled and picked it up. This was why she'd taken the risk and set herself up as bait: to protect Will and the girls.

"How long were you hunting us?" LaRouche asked.

She snapped her attention to him and straightened. "What?"

"We know you're FBI. We also know you're unstable, which makes this whole—" he motioned with his hand "—overmedication work seamlessly into our plans."

She swayed, gripping the bars. "You can't—"

"We already have. The drug will be released to the general public next month."

It was having a quicker effect on Sara than she'd expected. She struggled to find her words, make sense of the thoughts going through her brain.

"How did you get it…get it through testing?" she asked.

Her eyelids felt heavy and her legs weakened.

"There she goes," Harrington said.

Collapsing on the floor, she stared up at the bright ceiling lights. A low hum filled her ears. She held the photograph so she could see it.

Will. Will and his emerald eyes.

She would die without telling him she loved him. And more innocent people would die because Sara had failed.

"People will die!" she gasp-shouted.

"Well, you will anyway."

She closed her eyes, wanting them gone, wanting her last few moments on earth to be filled with the image of Will and his girls.

"Sa-ra, oh, Sa-ra," LaRouche said.

"Let's go," Harrington said.

"Wait, I've got to leave this."

"Come on, come on, already," Harrington said.

Sara had no idea what LaRouche had put in the cell and didn't care. She wanted them to leave so she could open her eyes and gaze upon the photograph of a smiling father and his two precious girls.

A door slammed and she opened her eyes. They were gone.

She crawled to the toilet, hoping to make herself throw up. Gray fog blurred her vision. She gasped, gripping the photograph in her hand. Willing herself to focus, she held the photograph close, struggled to see.

"Will," she whispered.

Will couldn't wait any longer. He tracked Nate down at Healthy Eats, where Will demanded to see Sara. Nate seemed worn down, probably from the gunshot wound, and he finally gave in. Will felt bad about pressuring his friend, but he needed to see Sara.

When Will and Nate arrived at the police station, the front office was empty.

"Spike?" Nate said.

Will started toward the cell area and Nate yanked him back. "Hang on a second."

Nate went to the computer and punched a couple of keys. A visual of the cell came up on the screen.

Sara was passed out on the floor.

"We've got to—"

Nate put up his hand to silence Will. Then he rewound

the video feed and played it back. There, on the screen, they watched Victor LaRouche shove something into Sara's mouth.

Nate pushed Will aside and went to unlock the door to the cell area.

"Sara," Will said. "Sara, wake up."

Nate unlocked the cell door and called for an ambulance.

"This is Detective Walsh. Send an ambulance to Echo Mountain Police Station immediately. I've got an unconscious female."

Will rushed to Sara's side and felt for a pulse. "Nate, we can't wait for an ambulance." He noticed a pill bottle on the cell floor. "Grab that and follow me," Will ordered.

He picked her up and marched out of the cell. When they got into the front office, Spike came in from the back. He was covered in dirt and carried a fire extinguisher.

"Where were you?" Nate said.

"A car fire out back. I locked up."

"Sit behind this desk and don't move until I tell you to."

"Yes, sir."

Nate opened the door for Will. "Let's get her to the hospital."

Will squeezed his hands together in prayer. *Please, God, please let her wake up. Let her be okay.*

They'd given her a drug to counteract the pill LaRouche had shoved down her throat, and the doctor said the next twenty-four hours were critical.

So Will sat beside her bed. And prayed.

She'd been still all night, hardly stirring, barely breathing.

He closed his eyes and continued to pray. Will couldn't lose her this way. He couldn't lose her, period. He hadn't felt this kind of connection since Megan.

Who would have thought he'd fall in love with a woman like Sara? The FBI agent was determined first and foremost, and had a protective instinct that would scare off a hardened criminal. Such instincts would come in handy with his precocious daughters. That was, *if* Sara had any interest in a future with Will and the girls.

Was he assuming too much? Was he the only one who felt the dynamic pull between them, the trust growing each and every day they spent together? He hoped he wasn't imagining things.

"You're praying."

He snapped his eyes open. Sara stared at him with a confused frown.

"And you're awake," he said, reaching out to take her hand.

"I'm not dead?" she said, with surprise in her voice.

"We got you to the hospital in time."

"LaRouche and Harrington?"

"The truth is out. Nate's got LaRouche on video, forcing you to take the pill. They thought they'd destroyed it, but Nate had a second feed going to another server, courtesy of Zack Carter, who also retrieved the video off your phone."

"That's great news."

"There's more. David Price decided to tell the truth. He gave the feds evidence against LaRouche and Harrington."

"Wow, all this while I was asleep. Did Nate ever figure out how they got to Petrellis?"

"LaRouche and Harrington tracked him down through employee records and bribed him to kidnap you."

"That poor guy. He was collateral damage."

"The ladies at Echo Mountain Church are planning a fund-raiser to support his wife's care."

"That's awfully nice. Think he'll go to jail?"

"Nate's pushing for community service. But be assured, LaRouche and Harrington are going to jail for a very long time."

"It's over." She sighed. "Finally."

Silence stretched between them. The case may be over, but there was more to discuss.

"Sara—"

"Thanks for stopping by." She pulled her hand from his.

"That sounds like a dismissal."

"You should go."

"Excuse me?"

"Will, I'm in the hospital because I was given an overdose of a medication that could have killed me. This is what I do for a living. I pursue violent offenders. That kind of ugliness has no place in your life."

"You're going back to the FBI? I thought you were suspended."

"After everything that's happened, especially the lengths I went to to nail LaRouche and Harrington, I think Bonner will offer me my position back."

"Sara, there are other ways to fight for justice that don't involve throwing yourself into the line of fire."

She interlaced her hands together, making it impossible for Will to hold them again. "You don't really know me, Will. You know only a fragment of what I am—the fragile woman who needed to be rescued from the mountains. But I know you. I see the wonderful life you have with two precious girls, and a community that cares about you. You need a woman who will stay home and bake cookies and draw pictures with your daughters. That's not me."

He took a chance. He had to. "How do you know if you've never tried?"

Sara sighed and shook her head. "You should go home, be with your family."

"After you answer me one last question, and I need to know so I don't keep messing things up."

"Okay."

"I wasn't imagining it, was I?" he said, his voice hoarse. "This thing between us?"

"Adrenaline. We were swimming in it most of the time we were together. It's to be expected that you'd confuse it with something else."

"You never felt anything—" he hesitated "—when I did this?"

Leaning forward, he pressed a gentle kiss on her lips. When he pulled back, her eyes watered with unshed tears.

"Of course I felt something," she said. "That's why you need to leave." She turned her back to him. "I wish you and the girls the very best."

Will started to reach out and stopped himself. He couldn't force her to open her heart to the glorious possibilities of love, of making a life with Will and the girls. Yet she'd admitted to feeling something, which meant she loved him, right?

Determined. Wasn't that one of her finest qualities? In this case he sensed she was determined that Will find a better woman than Sara.

There was no better woman than Sara, not for Will anyway. How could he convince her of that?

He pressed a light kiss against her head. "I love you, Sara Vaughn. God bless."

SEVENTEEN

Two days later, Sara was released from the hospital and moved into the Echo Mountain Resort at the request of Detective Walsh. Although the case against LaRouche and Harrington seemed solid, Nate wanted Sara to stay in town until they resolved some issues.

The longer she stayed, the harder it would be to leave, especially because of the gifts Will and the girls dropped off at the front desk for her: chocolates, homemade cookies she assumed were snicker poodles and drawings. There were drawings of Will and the girls, drawings of the mountains and drawings of Will and Sara holding hands.

She sighed. If only…

And why not? Why couldn't you be happy here with Will and the girls?

She grabbed her phone and pressed the number for her boss at the FBI, but didn't hit Send. He'd left her a few messages asking her to call him back and discuss her situation.

A part of her had no interest in whatever he had to say, even if he offered an apology and her job back. After spending the week with the people of Echo Mountain, she saw what true loyalty looked like, loyalty and trust. For whatever reason, she'd never developed that kind of relationship with her peers or supervisors at work. They hadn't even trusted her enough to share critical information about their investigation of David Price—which would have prevented this entire disaster.

The lack of trust was partially her fault. Up to this point

in life she rarely trusted anyone, yet if you didn't trust, you couldn't expect people to trust you in return.

Then there was Will.

She placed her phone on the table and gazed out the window.

Who would have thought a man like Will would have helped her see the world differently, taught her to trust and work as a team? She could take that lesson back with her to the FBI, which would make her a better agent.

For some reason, she couldn't make the call.

"What is wrong with you?" she muttered.

A knock sounded at the door. She crossed the hotel room and welcomed Nate. "Hey, come on in."

Nate, arm in a sling, entered her room.

"How's the shoulder?" she asked.

"Less irritating than yesterday."

"And the shooter?"

"Alive, and talking once he heard LaRouche and Harrington had been arrested. He'd been on their payroll for years as an enforcer."

"A drug company needing an enforcer. That says it all." She shook her head. "How's the investigation going?"

Nate noticed her neatly folded clothes in an open suitcase. "Why, you in a hurry to leave town?"

"I guess." She went back to the window. Bree and a young man were putting up Christmas lights along the split rail fence.

Christmas, the holiday she never celebrated because she was alone, because she thought spending it with her little brother would only remind him of everything they'd lost.

"It doesn't work, ya know," Nate said.

She turned to him. "I'm sorry?"

"Running."

"Not sure what you mean."

"I recognize that look in your eye. I used to see it when

I looked in the mirror. So I ran, thinking it would go away." He shrugged. "It didn't."

"I'm not sure I know what—"

"Will Rankin."

"What about him?"

"You'll regret it."

She tore her gaze from Nate's and changed the subject. "You think the case is solid against LaRouche and Harrington?"

"One hundred percent. I've gotta ask—what were you thinking swallowing that pill?"

"I'd hoped to fake it, but well, you saw the video. LaRouche got hold of me."

"Why agree to take it in the first place?"

"They threatened to hurt Will and the girls."

"Ah, right, go after the people you love as leverage."

Her gaze shot up to meet his.

"I'm a detective, remember?" He winked. "I know Will fell fast and hard, but I wasn't as sure about you—" he hesitated "—until just now. Wish you'd reconsider abandoning him. The guy's been through a lot."

"It's better this way."

"Better for whom?" he challenged.

Her phone rang and she eyed the caller ID. "My boss," she said, to put an end to her conversation with Nate.

"I'll see what I can do about letting you leave town," he said. He opened the door and turned. "Too bad, though. Chief Washburn is retiring and they've offered me his job. I could use a seasoned detective on my team."

"I'm sure you'll have plenty of officers fighting for that spot."

"None with the experience of a federal agent."

Nate left and she went back to the window. Light snow dusted the grounds with the spirit of Christmas. Bree looked up and waved at Sara. Sara waved back and smiled. Then Sara glanced at Claire's and Marissa's drawings on the dining table. Another smile tugged at the corner of her lips. She wasn't used to all this smiling.

Sara fingered one of the drawings and noticed writing on the backside. She turned it over…

And read a Bible quote written in Will's hand: "Hope deferred makes the heart sick, but a longing fulfilled is a tree of life." Proverbs 13:12.

Sara's phone beeped, indicating another missed call. Her boss. Rather than call him back and make a rash decision that would affect the rest of her life, she decided to try something radical, for her anyway.

She kneeled beside the bed, clasped her hands together and opened her heart to God's love, praying for guidance, and maybe even…forgiveness.

Will hadn't seen Sara in the past few days, but he knew she was staying at the resort. His friend, resort manager Aiden McBride, told Will that she rarely left her room.

Will had to stop thinking about her and let nature take its course. Sara must come to peace in her own way, in her own time. When she did, Will hoped, he prayed, she'd find her way back to him.

Tonight, as they waited for the town's Christmas tree to light up, as it would every Saturday through Christmas, he ached for Sara to be here with him and the girls.

"What time is it, Daddy?" Marissa said, smiling as she stared at the tree.

"Almost time, sweetie pie," he said.

Claire squeezed his other hand. "Can we get cider after the tree lighting?"

"Sounds like a great idea."

"And roasted checker nuts?" Marissa asked.

"They're called chestnuts, not checker nuts," Claire said, rolling her eyes.

"I like checker nuts." Marissa pouted.

"So do I," his mother-in-law said, stepping up beside them.

She smiled at Will, actually smiled.

"Hi, Mary," Will said, giving her a hug.

"I like chocolate more than checker—I mean, chestnuts," Claire said.

"We'll get you some of that, too, if you'd like," Mary said.

"Really? You said sugar makes us hyper," Claire said.

"A little sugar at Christmastime won't hurt." Mary smiled at her granddaughters.

"She came, she came to the tree lighting!" Marissa took off into the crowd.

"Wait, Marissa, hang on." Will ran after her, while Mary hung back with Claire.

Eyes on his daughter's bright pink jacket, he didn't even notice what had gotten her all excited until he was face-to-face with Sara.

"Hi, Miss Sara! Merry Christmas!" Marissa said, hugging her. Sara kneeled and hugged Marissa back.

Will was speechless, unsure what to think. She'd kept to herself, locked in her hotel room for the past five days, yet she was here, standing right in front of him.

Sara stood. "Hi," she said to Will.

"Hello."

"Give her a hug, Daddy," Marissa encouraged.

Before he could reach for her, Sara wrapped her arms around his waist and leaned against his chest. He held her then, squeezed her tight so that he could remember this moment forever, because it could be just that, a moment.

He breathed in her scent, a mix of vanilla and cinnamon, and realized he'd always think of Sara at the holidays.

"Claire, Claire, look!" Marissa motioned to her sister.

Will released Sara, who greeted his eldest daughter. "Hi, Claire, it's so good to see you."

"You, too, Miss Sara," Claire said.

"Merry Christmas, Sara," Mary said. "Girls, how about we find Papa at the hot-cocoa table."

"Cocoa! Cocoa! Cocoa!" Marissa clapped, jumping up and down.

"Calm down." Claire rolled her eyes again.

The girls grabbed on to their grandmother's hands and waded through the crowd.

"Wow, your mother-in-law actually wished me a Merry Christmas," Sara said.

"I guess she was impressed that you were willing to die to protect me and the girls."

She looked at him in question.

"Nate told us why you took the drug in the first place."

"Wow, word really gets around."

He shrugged. "Small town."

A moment of uncomfortable silence passed between them, then he asked the question he dreaded hearing the answer to. "When do you go back?"

"To work?"

He nodded.

"I'm not going back."

Could this mean…?

"Why not?" he asked.

"I'm leaving the FBI."

Hope swelled in his chest. "What about catching the bad guys?"

"I can do that from anywhere." She hesitated. "Like here, maybe?"

"You mean…?"

She shrugged. "Echo Mountain, if that's okay with you."

"Really?" he said in disbelief.

"Unless you think it's a bad idea."

"No, it's a great idea. What changed your mind?"

She slipped her hand into his. "A very wise man told me I could fight for justice in ways other than throwing myself into the line of fire."

"Sounds like a brilliant man," he teased.

"I guess that's why I fell in love with him, huh?" She offered a tender smile.

"Aw, honey, I am blessed beyond words," he said, and kissed her, right there, in front of the entire community of Echo Mountain.

Applause broke out around them, and they both smiled, breaking the kiss. Friends patted him on the back, offering congratulations and warm wishes.

All he could see was Sara, the woman he loved.

The Christmas tree suddenly lit up, bathing the crowd in an array of color. The group burst into song—"Joy to the World."

Will and Sara shared a knowing smile.

"They're playing your song," she teased.

"No, sweetheart, it's our song."

* * * * *

Dear Reader,

Trust is a complicated belief that can cause a myriad of emotions. Sometimes, when we've been betrayed, we find it hard to trust and love, afraid to risk being hurt again.

Single father Will Rankin lost his young wife to cancer a few years ago, and now aches for a connection, a connection to a woman who will also be a nurturing force in his young daughters' lives. What he does not expect is to be drawn to a woman he rescues, an FBI agent determined never to trust or love again. Her only goal: justice, even at great personal cost.

Sara Vaughn experienced tragedy at a very young age, and has closed herself off to the very idea of love. Yet Will is a compassionate and determined man, who sees the possibilities for Sara to ease out of the darkness and into the light.

Through their journey we learn that no matter how deep a person's emotional wounds, through compassion and love we can find our way back to grace. And yes, we can even learn to trust and love again. There's no better time to be reminded of this lesson than at Christmas.

Peace,

Hope White